Petunia PERRY

and the

CURSE of

the UGLY

PigeoN

Pamela BUTCHART

nosy crow

Illustrated by GEMMA CORRELL

For Perrine

First published in the UK in 2015 by Nosy Crow Ltd
The Crow's Nest, 10a Lant Street
London, SE1 1QR, UK

Nosy Crow and associated logos are trademarks and/or registered
trademarks of Nosy Crow Ltd

A CIP catalogue record for this book is available from the British Library.

Printed and bound in the UK by Clays Ltd, St. Ives Plc
Typeset by Tiger Media, Bishops Stortford, Hertfordshire

Papers used by Nosy Crow are made from wood grown in
sustainable forests

ISBN: 978 0 85763 488 7

To: Epic Records

From: Peri

(Real name inflicted by parents = Petunia. Why would they do this? What did I ever do to them?)

Date: 6th November

Time: 2am (I may have insomnia)

Place: My wardrobe

Age: Recently turned 12 (it was weird – you'll soon see why)

Mood: In desperate need of a Mars bar (but I'd settle for a Twix)

Best friend: Cammy (even though I'm 100% sure she hates me, and 93.5% sure I saw her making a voodoo doll of me In Food Technology today)

I love: Ham. Pugs. NOT being accused of spoon theft

You love: I'm sure that's your own private business, but please insert here if you wish:_____

_____

Margaret's advice: Unavailable (FYI: Margaret is a cat. She is also awesome)

Issues: (1) Possible lack of oxygen due to confined space. (2) I know that this will make you just as sad and angry as me, Epic Records, but I need to tell you that the most unique band (ever!) recently split because my band mate Cammy won't speak to me (she thinks I blabbed her weird name-secret, which I kind of did, but it was an accident!). This now means that I am bandless and friendless, and that YOU have missed out on being our label. Epic Records, I know that this won't be easy to hear, but our band had a cat in it. THAT'S how unique it was!

Next steps: I have decided that I am going to deal with this situation by writing my memoirs (since I am no longer in the band once deemed the "Next Big Thing" by Cammy's mum).

Thanks for listening.

Try not to let this break you.

Yours sincerely

Petunia Perry

PETUNIA PERRY AND THE CURSE OF THE UGLY PIGEON - A MEMOIR

SOME IMPORTANT INFORMATION BEFORE WE START

My grossly under-deodorised English teacher says it's important to "set the scene" when beginning a story, so I shall now tell you that while I write this I am sitting in my wardrobe with a torch, like someone at sea in an old movie. You may think it's weird that I'm sitting in a wardrobe. Or you may have just assumed that I am mega-rich and have one of those huge walk-in, room-sized wardrobes that you could easily fit a call-centre inside. If you are thinking either of these things then you are wrong because:

1 It is not weird (unusual, yes, but not weird). Because it said on the Internet that if you

3

want to be a serious writer, you must have a separate "writing room". My writing room is a wardrobe with a small chair in it (we all have to start somewhere). Although it's quite cramped, Mum's winter coats (which she INSISTS on keeping in MY wardrobe) are actually quite comfortable (even though they smell of Old).

2 I am *not* rich. Far from it! Mum makes us walk everywhere, even though we own a car. I can only assume we are too poor to buy petrol as I do not buy her "health reasons" excuse. I suppose she is only being a good mother who is just trying to shield me from the knowledge of our poverty. Whatever happens, I am NOT having another car-boot sale to make money. Regardless of what

Dad says, I still believe that's how I got chicken pox.

3 I am hiding away in my wardrobe because I can never show my human face to the world ever again after all of the horrific-ness that has happened recently.

I am also writing in a wardrobe because apparently my bedroom is a public area. Dad came into my room earlier and asked me what I was writing (he is a man of no boundaries). Then he tried to tell me that memoirs are for people who have died. I told him I expect to die of humiliation any day now. He said that that was "DEAD FUNNY". And then he cracked up for about twenty minutes.

I did not know I was living with a comedy genius.

Note to reader: That was sarcasm. It is very important that you understand sarcasm and have (hopefully) already started to practise it. If you did not get this, then you are probably too young to be reading my memoirs. You no doubt still think your mum and dad are "great", and might well be sat in a paddling pool full of colourful plastic balls. But please keep reading anyway. It will prepare you for what's coming (chronic humiliation by parents, for which there is no cure).

A Bit About Me

It feels a bit stupid putting a "Bit About Me" section in here, you know, since these are *my* memoirs, and are therefore *all* about me. But I suppose it's important that before we start, you know something about who I am and what my beef is with my mum and dad. I suppose you'll also probably want to know why my best friend was making a voodoo doll of me in Food Technology.

OK. So…

1. Who am I?

I am Petunia Perry (but everyone calls me Peri). Please read on for the full (weird) story.

2. Where am I?

I've almost made it through my first term at Fortress Academy.

3. What is my beef with my parents?

They are my parents.

Normal Parents = Occasionally embarrassing.

My Parents = Me sitting in a wardrobe doing this.

4. Why did your best friend make a voodoo doll of you in Food Technology?

Because she thinks I told everyone about her "Deep, Dark Secret". Then everything got a little out of hand, because (awful) Jessica Clark got involved, turned Cammy against me and completely ruined our chance of worldwide cat-band fame!

conclusion

My best friend will most likely never speak to me *ever* again. Our dreams of band fame and possible musical world domination are over. And my mum is probably sitting downstairs right now flicking through *Every Parent's Guide to Total Offspring Humiliation Part 2* for inspiration.

Welcome to the tragic life of me, Petunia Perry.

WELCOME TO THE MADNESS OF SECONDARY SCHOOL

LESSON — BEWARE OF BLACK BANANAS

Note to reader: I have decided to sometimes include a "lesson" in my memoirs. Hopefully this will help you (the reader) to avoid potentially cringeful or even full-blown humiliating situations.

Everything began to go wrong when we started at Fortress Academy. When me and Cammy were in primary school, there never even used to be an "I'm-so-great-I-poop-diamonds" group *or* an "ugly-pigeon-person" group. Life was much easier back then, when people used to be judged on important things, like how far you could swing back on your chair without cracking your skull open, or who could

9

win a semi-final staring competition, or who was sick enough to do the "Sick-Lick" (which is when someone dares you to lick someone else's nose for a pound). These were simpler and, I would argue, better times.

I remember the time Lewis Draper challenged Sally Gold to a "Black Banana Eating Contest" because he had heard that Sally Gold was too scared to eat the black bits and that she always left the last three centimetres of her banana to avoid potential spider's eggs.

Apparently, Sally Gold saw a programme that said sometimes spiders lay their eggs in the bottom of bananas, and if you eat them, thousands of spiders hatch inside you, and then you die. But it turned out that Lewis Draper had been given "unreliable information" by Max Martin (who claims to have a pet unicorn) and it WASN'T Sally Gold who was scared of bananas, it was Jeff Jones.

So anyway, a note was sent round our primary school telling everyone to save their bananas from the canteen until the day of the challenge. So we did. And everyone made sure they picked the spottiest banana from the fruit bowl every day for two weeks. I even saw some people punching their bananas to make sure they went all bruised and squishy.

Then when the day of the "Black Banana Eating Contest" came, Lewis Draper went first and put his hand into the "Black Banana Bag" and pulled out a medium-bad one (it was covered in tiny brown dots, but had no obvious big black bits) and everyone went, "OooooOOOO" (which meant he was lucky because we all knew what was lurking in there). Then it was Sally's turn, and she pulled out a medium bad one too.

They were both quite lucky for a while because they kept getting OK-ish ones. But then when they had both eaten about four bananas each, Lewis pulled out "THE BLACK BEAST". (And the rule is that you're not allowed to put any bananas back, so you HAVE to eat The Black Beast if you get it, or you lose.)

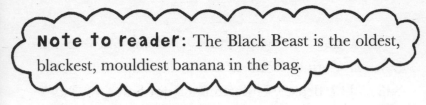

Note to reader: The Black Beast is the oldest, blackest, mouldiest banana in the bag.

So we all watched as Lewis peeled the rotten skin back slowly. The banana was even blacker inside than it was on the outside. Lewis raised it to his mouth, but then he must have caught a whiff of it because he started to gag. And then he said he couldn't do it, and that he was going to be sick.

So we all started cheering, "Sall-Y, Sall-Y, Sall-Y!" because this meant that Sally Gold was the new Black Banana Champion. But then Sally grabbed The Black Beast out of Lewis's hand and ate it all in one bite. And that's when everyone stopped cheering, and we all felt a bit sick. And to this day, nobody knows why she did it because she had already won.

After that, everyone stopped doing the "Black Banana Eating Contest" and now everyone calls Sally "The Beast". Unfortunately for Sally, the Black Banana story spread fast (since it *was* pretty shocking) and it wasn't long before everyone at all the other schools in our area knew about "The Beast" too. Cammy even said that her cousin heard the story at *his* school, and he lives in Ireland!

So there you go. I guess bad news really *does* travel fast. So as soon as we started at Fortress (and the pointless popularity-rating began) Sally was automatically placed in the least-popular group (even though she is the current "Black Banana Eating Champion"!). Popularity is messed up. I mean, one minute you're an absolute legend, then before anyone can say, "Please-don't-eat-that-it's-clearly-diseased" you're an outcast, forced to eat your lunch on your own in the long grass. Like a gorilla.

Anyway, as I was saying, instead of being judged on guts and bravery and cleverness, some "genius" decided that once we get to secondary school, we should all be judged on stupid, non-important things like hair, and smell, and teeth. And then put into "groups". So really, secondary school is just like a fancy dog show. But with people. And less peeing against table legs (depending on which school you go to).

And then the whole "Ugly Pigeon" thing started!

THE WHOLE UGLY PIGEON THING

LESSON – <u>NEVER</u> TURN UP TO A PIGEON FUNERAL WITHOUT A CHEESE SANDWICH

Note to reader: The "Ugly Pigeon" was a pigeon that used to terrorise everyone when we first started at Fortress.

The Ugly Pigeon was obsessed with cheese sandwiches, and if you had one, and it saw you, you were in for it. The Ugly Pigeon would run at you, flap its scabby wings and screech until you gave in and dropped your lunch. I didn't even know that

15

pigeons could screech like that until I stupidly got a cheese sandwich and took it outside.

The Ugly Pigeon had loads of feathers missing and scars because it used to fight with the seagulls and crows for all the playground leftovers (and I'm pretty sure I saw it with a weapon one time). Then one day, someone noticed that it hadn't been around for a while, and that's when the rumours started. Some people said it was dead, some people said it had gone to terrorise another school, and Max Martin said he saw Mr Lump take it home to be his pet when he retired last week. (Max Martin has "truth-telling" issues.)

Then someone came up with the worst thing ever – the Ugly Pigeon Wind. And everyone believed it, even Charles Wainsworth, who doesn't believe in ANYTHING spooky or supernatural and once had an argument with Miss Morgan (who teaches RE) for a whole period. At the end, Miss Morgan said that it hadn't been an argument, and that it had been a "discussion". But I didn't believe her because she looked like she wanted to smash his face in with her stapler.

Anyway, the Ugly Pigeon Wind became a thing

when three girls in our year started crying about it in PE. They said that they had walked past where the Ugly Pigeon used to "hunt" and they had felt a "breeze". And that the "breeze" had felt weird and they just *knew* it was the spirit of the Ugly Pigeon.

Then a few other girls started crying too, and before you know it, there was this sort of "vigil" thing in the playground with candles and flowers, and one girl had even drawn a picture of the Ugly Pigeon and put it in a frame. Then a sign was put up that said there was going to be a memorial service the next day at lunch (and that gifts were optional).

So me and Cammy went along, because it seemed like the right thing to do. There were loads of people there, and they were all telling stories about how "loveable" and "sweet" the Ugly Pigeon had been. Then at the end people started laying down cheese sandwiches, and I felt *terrible* because we hadn't brought anything.

So Cammy searched in her bag and found some raisins, and we put those down. But that made people tut at us, as if to say, "The Ugly Pigeon would have HATED those! Why don't you just bring him back to life and KILL HIM AGAIN?!"

For about a week after the service, people kept sitting beside the Ugly Pigeon's shrine and leaving their crusts behind at lunch. But after a while everyone kind of forgot about it all until Jessica Clark (uurgghh) came to school one day with a permed mullet and blamed it on the Ugly Pigeon.

At first people were shocked. The "U.P." had become a bit of a legend at our school and no one likes a fallen hero. But then everyone quickly started to agree with Jessica (since she's the most popular girl in our year and therefore powerful).

Jessica said that she had accidentally stood on a crust when she walked past the Ugly Pigeon's shrine on her way to the hairdresser. Then Jessica said that when she was getting her hair cut she had felt the Ugly Pigeon Wind and knew that the Ugly Pigeon had followed her to the hairdresser and cursed her hair and turned it into a permed mullet. One of Jessica's friends dared to suggest that it might've just been a hairdryer Jessica felt. Now that poor girl eats lunch with "The Beast".

Shortly after Jessica's permed mullet experience, everyone decided that the Ugly Pigeon was an "evil presence". And that his evil spirit was haunting the school, trying to make everyone just as ugly as he had once been.

So the shrine was promptly dismantled and people stopped wearing their "R.I.P. U.P." badges.

I felt a bit sorry for the Ugly Pigeon, but at least people were finally acknowledging that this bird hadn't exactly been nice when it was alive. I think the Ugly Pigeon would have wanted to be remembered exactly as he was (a terror).

A girl called Hectoria was the first "official" curse victim of the Ugly Pigeon (after it was somehow decided that what had happened to Jessica didn't count, and that in fact, her "experience" had given her some sort of "sixth sense" that allowed her to see who was *really* cursed by the Ugly Pigeon).

Me and Cammy found Hectoria crying next to her locker after Jessica had drawn the Ugly Pigeon symbol on it in pink lipstick. So I suggested Hectoria dress up as an actual pigeon and chase Jessica and the rest of the "populars" around school with real pigeon poo on a stick. Cammy even offered to help her collect the poo! But Hectoria decided that the best thing to do would be to straighten her hair, start wearing her mum's make-up to school and burn her days-of-the-week tights (which was a tragedy because on the first week of secondary school Hectoria wore her Friday tights on a Thursday by mistake, and Mr Hanson let us leave school early because he thought it was Friday – it was brilliant!).

I stopped feeling sorry for Hectoria shortly after I became the second victim. It was horrible. I came out of History to find a HUGE Ugly Pigeon had been drawn on my locker. Everyone was laughing and pointing and "coo-coo-ing" at me (which was mortifying AND factually inaccurate, since the Ugly Pigeon did not "coo-coo" – he screeched). I should have known then that I was cursed.

So, after the whole "being-crowned-U.P. thing" by the horrible girls in our year, that's when me and Cammy made a pact that no matter how mean, giggly-ly, hair-straightener-y and BORING all the girls in our year became under Jessica's rule, we would NOT run home and put our mum's make-up on or burn fantastic and helpful legwear. We would resist.

Cammy called it "having bones". Which I *think* means the same as "having guts". It's sometimes hard to understand Cammy. She's a bit weird – in a good way (well, most of the time).

Then Cammy made us both sign the "Declaration of Self Independence", which said stuff like:

- We will be ourselves and stay EXACTLY the same as we were in primary school.
- We will still do ALL the fun things we've always done (Metal Detector Tuesdays, for example, will live on forever!).
- We will NOT wear lip gloss, straighten our hair or use fancy shampoo (but we will wear deodorant).
- We will refer to the "populars" as the "poopulars".
- We will do whatever we want, just like we always have, even if it's not what other people do.
- We will never EVER stop being best friends and we will never EVER let anything or anyone break the band of our friendship!

The moment I signed it Cammy literally started screaming. I looked up and saw that she was smiling and tugging her hair (yes, I'm aware that this is not normal behaviour, but that's just Cammy). But I knew EXACTLY what was happening. Cammy had just had a FANTASTICALABULOUS idea (which is what we call ideas when words like "fantastic" and "brilliant" just aren't enough).

I could see that Cammy was struggling to verbalise the idea. Her mouth was trying to do – well, something, and her arms were waving all over the place. This idea was BIG.

"You OK, Cammy?" I asked, trying to remember the first-aid training we'd had in Year 6. But then all of a sudden Cammy grabbed a pen and started DRAWING ON HER BEDROOM WALL. That's how serious this was.

I watched as she manically scrawled over her Harry Potter wallpaper. At first I thought she might write, "HELP! I'M CHOKING!" but she didn't. She began drawing what looked like a fried egg on Dumbledore's forehead. Then she began merging his eyes together and giving them legs. And that's when I realised she was drawing a guitar. But it wasn't until she turned Harry's scar into a saxophone (Cammy is quite skilled with a marker pen) that I realised what her FANTASTICALABULOUS idea was.

She wanted us to start a band!

CAMEMBERT STINKS!

LESSON – DON'T NAME YOUR CHILDREN AFTER CHEESE

Cammy and I weren't always best friends. I mean, we were always *friends* but we never used to be proper (capital letters) Best Friends.

It happened during a Year 5 school trip to see the worst film in the world. That was the day our best friendshipness was sealed.

Cammy says it was fate, but I'm pretty certain it was the cheese.

Note to reader: Cammy's full name is Camembert. In case you don't know, Camembert is also the name of a rather stinkful French cheese (Cammy's mum's a bit weird).

Sometimes people make fun of Cammy, like the time she did Show and Tell in the style of an opera, rather than just saying it in a normal voice like everyone else. But that's just Cammy.

Cammy doesn't usually care if people at school laugh at her. The only thing that REALLY upsets her is when people make fun of her full name. Being called Camembert never used to bother her that much (probably because most people in Year 5 don't know what it is). But that all changed the day Robb Silverman caused a "scene" at the cinema.

OK, so what happened is our old teacher (Mr Fran) wanted us to see "history in action" so he took us all to some film about the Victorians (which was terrible). The only good thing about going on the trip was that Mr Fran had said we could bring snacks with us (and I LOVE snacks).

Mum never buys good snacks like chocolate or popcorn unless it's a special occasion (like Christmas, my birthday or when she's ready to "take her boss's life"). But for some strange, unknown reason, this trip to the cinema to see an educational film was deemed by Mum to be a "special occasion". I thought this was a bit weird, but hey, why argue!

So anyway, Cammy brought snacks too. However, Cammy's mum is a bit of a foodie and likes really weird things like olives and anchovies, and she absolutely *loves* CAMEMBERT CHEESE. And (unfortunately) this food-weirdness has rubbed off on Cammy.

So when the film started Cammy pulled a full cheeseboard out of her bag (it even had a little bunch of grapes on the side!). And as soon as she cut into the Camembert, this terrible, sweet-yet-pungently-horrid smell escaped. Cammy didn't seem to notice. But Robb Silverman did. He was sitting in front of us and he started screaming, "OH MY GOD! Was that you? *WAS THAT YOU?!*" to the boy sitting next to him.

Then all the boys started blaming each other, and holding their noses, while Cammy just sat there slicing away, completely unaware that the smell was coming from her.

That's when Mr Fran came rushing up the steps to see what all the fuss was about, and told everyone to "Pipe down!"

And then he said, "Stop it! It's just Camembert. Camembert's a smelly cheese." And then he pointed

RIGHT AT CAMMY.

I couldn't believe it.

Why didn't he just take Cammy's cheese knife and stab her in the back with it?

That would have been less painful!

Robb Silverman and the rest of the boys stared at Mr Fran with their mouths wide open. And then they all looked at Cammy and burst out laughing.

For weeks after that everyone held their nose when Cammy walked past them in the corridor, and burst out laughing when her name was read out on the register and chanted "Sme-lly-CHEESE! Sme-lly

CHEESE!" at her at least fifty times a day.

You see, the tragic thing was that Robb Silverman and the rest of the boys didn't realise that Mr Fran had been talking about the CHEESE being smelly. They thought Mr Fran had actually called CAMMY a smelly cheese!

Mr Fran became quite popular after that, and when we were getting off the bus that day, Robb Silverman patted him on the back and called him a "legend".

And to make a really bad situation even worse, Mr Fran took being called a "legend" the wrong way, and I guess he felt all "inspired" or something because the next week he took us all to see a THREE-HOUR-LONG play about "Roman times". But thankfully this time Cammy just took an apple.

So anyway, on the bus going home after the "incident" I decided to take Cammy's mind off the fact that Robb Silverman kept squeezing his face between the space in the seats in front of us and whispering, "I bet your feet smell like Cheddar, don't they?" I did this by deciding to share a secret with her that I had never shared with anyone.

That's when I told Cammy that my real name

is Petunia, and that through a series of (bizarre but fortunate) events, I'd managed to hide it from everyone for years.

"But Petunia's a nice name," Cammy whispered when I told her.

"So is Camembert," I lied.

"No it's not," she said. "It's a cheese, Peri. But thanks." And she was right, so I just smiled and didn't say anything.

"So," whispered Cammy, looking excited. "Tell me how you've kept it a secret!" And then she pushed our jackets into the space between the seats in front to block out Robb Silverman's face.

HOW I CAME TO BE NICKNAMED "PERI PERRY"

I told Cammy that on the first day of primary school three things happened:

1 I was permanently crushed (emotionally) by one of the office ladies.

2 I was saved from a life of "Petunia" name-bullying by the very same office lady.

3 I ended up being called "Peri Perry", which, obviously, means I sometimes get weird looks.

I'd been sent to the office to collect the "First Ever New Reception Register". Our teacher, Mr Kenny, had said that I was very lucky to be chosen for such a Big Responsibility on the first day of school and he pointed down the hall towards the office and then shut the classroom door and totally abandoned me. I was terrified. I wasn't READY for a Big Responsibility. I was only five years old for grapes' sake! I didn't even know HOW to collect the register from the office.

I somehow managed to fumble my way down the corridor and find the office. But when I got there I couldn't reach up to the glass door bit where the office ladies were because I was too small. So I just stood there for about ten minutes before I eventually worked up the courage to knock on the wall underneath the glass window.

That's when the office lady who would scar me for life stuck her head out and peered down at me. And that's when I saw that she had a VERY weird eye.

I was already pretty fragile, having been given the scary responsibility and then abandoned by my teacher and everything, so when I saw the weird eye I just lost it and started bawling.

Weird-eye woman picked me up, pulled me right through the window into the office and sat me on her lap. I thought she was going to eat me.

"What's wrong, petal?" she asked.

Well, I couldn't tell her, could I?

So I just kept crying.

"What's your name, sweet pea?"

But I refused to tell her. If she knew my name she'd be able to find me if I escaped.

But she wouldn't give up.

"Why won't you tell me your name, honey?"

So that's when I began REALLY crying. You know, the kind of crying when you can't catch a breath and it sounds a bit like you're drowning in your own saliva, and before I even realised it I'd shouted, "No! Not my name. You can't know my name!"

"Is there something wrong with your name, darling?" weird-eye woman asked, looking concerned. "Is that why you're crying?"

I nodded that it was. I couldn't tell her it was the eye.

It worked. She released her grasp and sat me on the seat next to her. "OK, let me take a little look at your class register," she said as she began typing on her computer, and then she turned the screen to me and said, "Oh. This must be you. Is your name Petunia?"

I couldn't believe it. She was a witch.

"That's why you're crying, isn't it? Mr Kenny sent you to get the new Reception register. But you're scared that everyone is going to find out you're called Petunia and that they'll bully you because of your name, aren't you?"

I was stunned. I had NOT been worried about that at all! I didn't even know there was something wrong with my name! I was crushed. Scarred for life.

"Well, don't you worry, petal. I'll put a little note on the computer register next to your name that says not to call you Petunia. Now, let's see. What's short for Petunia? Hmmmm. Petty? No. Tunia? No, definitely not. What about Peri? It's not perfect, but it's a nice enough name. OK?"

I nodded that it was OK. I was still in shock.

"Good. I'll say that due to 'emotional reasons' the teachers should never, *ever* call you Petunia. There. Done. Now you don't have to worry about that ever again, Peri."

So I walked back to class, with a new name and a printout of the amended register.

Cammy looked confused. And then she said, "You'd think she would've changed your first name to something else so that you weren't called Peri Perry, wouldn't you?"

But before I could answer Cammy gasped and raised her hands to her mouth.

"Her weird eye!" she whispered. "She didn't notice your surname!"

And I nodded that she was correct.

And it was on that fateful, cheesy day in Year 5 that Cammy and I officially became best friends, bonded by the pain of our weird names.

NEW SCHOOL, NEW NAME

LESSON — ALWAYS HELP YOUR BEST FRIEND TO HIDE EMBARRASSING SECRETS!

By some miracle, when we moved up to secondary school, Robb Silverman (and a lot of the other boys/ disgustoids who'd witnessed the "Camembert's a Smelly Cheese" incident) went to a different school from us (probably one that specialises in boys with "problems"). And AMAZINGLY, by the time we started at Fortress, everybody else from our old school seemed to forget about the whole "Camembert" thing.

So that's when Cammy decided that there was NO WAY anyone at our new school could EVER find out that her real name was Camembert, because then someone would bring up the whole "Camembert's a smelly cheese" thing again.

Cammy calls it her Deep, Dark Secret. To be honest with you, I don't really think that Cammy's secret is THAT much of a big deal. I mean, it's pretty bad, but it's not "I eat seagull sandwiches" bad. But I would NEVER tell Cammy that. I mean, even though Cammy is usually completely and utterly oblivious to what people think of her, her Deep, Dark Secret REALLY bothers her. To use Cammy's exact words, she once said, "If anyone at Fortress ever finds out, I'll be forced to shave my head to divert their attention."

And I'm 100% sure that would work, but I don't really want her to be bald. So, to avoid anyone hearing Cammy's full name being read out in class, me and Cammy decided to have coughing/sneezing fits every time the teacher did the register.

That worked for the first two days at Fortress, but by day three our throats were hurting and people had started to move away from us in class. And I'm pretty sure I heard a rumour going round that me and Cammy had the plague.

Our situation reached breaking point when I had to spontaneously scream in the middle of Maths when one of the office ladies turned up at class and began to ask for Cammy by her full name.

We needed a new plan.

Cammy tried crying outside the school office, but instead of taking pity on her like Weird-Eye had done to me in Reception, they just sent her to the nurse.

So I suggested that we ask Cammy's mum to legally change her name, because I'd seen a programme that said as long as you paid a fee, you were allowed to change your name to anything you wanted (which is awesome, and means you could change your name to Cheese on Toast if you wanted, and it would be completely legal and everything!). But Cammy said that her mum wouldn't let her do that, and also that it would really hurt her feelings if she asked.

So, since I knew there was really nothing else we could do, I tried to cheer Cammy up by reminding her of the time we found the list of "Possible Baby Names" in her mum's favourite book, *The Super in Superstition*. I think my favourite possibility was Garlic.

Seriously.

GARLIC.

If that isn't grounds for murdering your parents in self-defence, then what is?!

But, unfortunately, Cammy could not be cheered. She said that she might as well be called Garlic because at least Garlic was "cooler" than Camembert because of garlic bread.

I didn't really agree with her on that one, but I decided not to say anything because I personally don't know what it's like to live with the fear of everyone chanting "Smelly Cheese" in your face.

But then on day four everything changed.

Cammy heard a rumour in her Latin class that there was this boy in Year 10 who was a "hacker" and that he could hack into the school's computer system and change things like a bad grade or a bad report before it was sent home (for the very reasonable fee of £20).

I didn't think £20 was a very reasonable fee at *all*, but Cammy said that you can't negotiate with criminals. And that we shouldn't try because The Hacker could be extremely dangerous. So Cammy made me give her all my pocket money (and some of my savings!) and together with her money (£2.75!) we had enough for the fee.

But then there was a problem. We didn't know who The Hacker was or how to find him because he had to keep his identity a secret. So we decided we'd ask someone in Year 10, and after being ignored by twelve people, flicked on the back of the head by four and handed a piece of used chewing gum by one, someone eventually felt sorry for us and answered our question.

This is what we found out:

Step 1: If you want The Hacker to do something for you, you have to go to the library and find a book called *Cement: A Complete Guide*.

Step 2: You write your message on a Post-it note in invisible ink (using the invisible-ink pen, which is buried in the plant pot next to the shelf) and then stick it on the last page of the book. Then put the book back on the shelf.

Step 3: Wait until 3.30pm. If The Hacker has

decided to help you, there will be a note in the back of the book.

So we did that, and then we waited until the end of the day. Then as soon as the bell rang we ran to the library and opened the book.

And there was a note:

Dear C,

Accepted.

Please insert £20 into the bag provided.

Give to my assistant, who will be browsing in the history section. She will be wearing a red hat.

Once payment is received your request shall be processed within 2 hours.

Destroy this note.

We looked up and saw a tiny girl wearing a red ladybird hat and mittens. She only looked about nine years old!

We walked over quickly and handed her the money. She inspected it carefully for ages, and then she put

the bag in her mitten and whispered, "Note?"

I pointed to Cammy, and Cammy opened her mouth and showed her.

"Excellent," whispered the ladybird girl. "Now, go." So we did.

The next day, me and Cammy sat sweating in registration. Our registration teacher had just read out "James Baxter" and Cammy was next.

"Maybe we should just cough anyway?" I said. "In case it's a scam?"

But Cammy just shook her head and gripped my hand even tighter under the desk. Her hand was sweating. Or maybe it was mine. It was hard to tell.

That's when I started to feel like everything had slowed down, and that Mr Burton was reading out the names in slooooooooow moooooooootion. I had to shut my eyes because I felt like I was going to pass out. And then he said it:

"CAMILLA PANCETTA BROWN?"

I couldn't believe it. It worked!

"CAMILLA? IS CAMILLA HERE?"

"Yes! Yes! I'm here. That's me! I'm Camilla!" said Cammy.

I stared at her in disbelief.

"Peri, can you believe it?" she whispered. "It worked!"

I wanted to ask why she hadn't bothered to change the "Pancetta" bit (since pancetta is basically bacon) but I didn't want to ruin the moment. I'm a good friend like that.

THE SPOONS

LESSON — RESPECT THE WISE WORDS OF YOUR ELDERS (ESPECIALLY IF THEY ARE WRITTEN IN CRUMBLINGLY OLD CHEMISTRY TEXT BOOKS)

After the whole "Ugly Pigeon" and "Hacker" dramas, things settled down for a couple of weeks, and me and Cammy spent most of our time working on band ideas!

Mr Dolderer's Chemistry class turned out to be a PERFECT place to work on our official band plans after we discovered a series of ancient instructions in an old textbook. The instructions were the kind you KNOW you really shouldn't follow because you're OBVIOUSLY being led into a trap by some smelly kid from 1995 who probably sat in the same seat you do now, licking the pages.

But everyone ALWAYS follows the instructions

(even though they pretend they don't). I'm not really sure why everyone does it; I mean, it's not like they don't know what's going to happen. I guess it's just a case of dazzlingly stupid curiosity, like when you touch the side of a BOILING HOT plate to see if it's hot almost immediately after the waitress has placed it down on the table in front of you and said, "Please be careful with the plate, it's BOILING HOT."

In case you're not familiar with the kind of "Textbook Instructions" to which I am referring, please see below:

Imagine you have just opened your textbook and turned to page six. At the bottom of page six, someone has scrawled: "Turn to page 18."

So you turn to page 18, even though you know you probably shouldn't.

And on page 18 someone has written: "Turn to page 56."

And then: "Turn to page 103."

And so on, and so on.

Until (after twenty or so pointless page turns) you reach the final page only to find the word: "SUCKER."

And that's basically it.

So a few weeks ago in Chemistry, Mr Dolderer handed me and Cammy what I am convinced must be the oldest textbook in the school. Part of the front cover pretty much dissolved in my hand as I held it, that's how old it was.

We were so shocked by the oldness of the textbook that we decided to search inside to find out just how old it actually was. And that's when we discovered that it was published in 1989! An antique!

Cammy rushed to the sink, put on a pair of rubber gloves and began turning the pages of the antique book VERY carefully. And then we found what we are convinced is the first EVER example of the "Turn to Page…" instruction game.

We followed the instructions, turning a LOT more pages than you usually have to when you're playing this game, and then Cammy turned to me and said, "I think this is a *real* one, Peri."

And I just KNEW that she was right, and that there was actually going to be some sort of SOMETHING at the end of this one.

And there was.

And it wasn't a ten-pound note taped to the page.

And it wasn't the answer to the meaning of life.

It was better.

It was basically a "Get Out of Chemistry" pass!!!

On the last page of the antique textbook, someone had drawn a tiny diagram showing the perfect seats to sit in if you wanted to avoid the eyes of Mr Dolderer. There was even a calculation next to the diagram showing how Mr Dolderer was too blind to see the last row of seats to the left of the room. Someone had even drawn beams coming out of Mr Dolderer's eyes and scrawled mathematical equations next to them calculating the impossibility of his weak eyes being able to see the last two seats in the back row

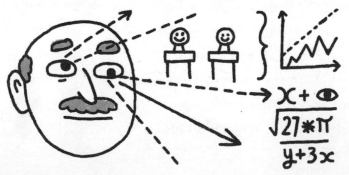

on the left.

Wonderfully, there was also a list of questions we could ask Mr Dolderer, such as, "Which is your favourite element and why?", which were apparently guaranteed to keep Mr Dolderer muttering away to himself for twenty-plus minutes while you had a snooze or got on with more important things.

So, since me and Cammy have Mr Dolderer three times a week, it only took us a couple of Chemistry lessons to come up with

THE BEST BAND IDEA EVER!

Cammy said that every time she watches one of those TV talent shows, the judges are always going on about looking for The Next Big Thing, and that this was EXACTLY what WE needed to be. But it wasn't as easy as that. I mean:

Number 1: Me and Cammy had no idea what The Next Big Thing was.

Number 2: We didn't seem to like the same music as each other.

Number 3: We couldn't play any instruments.

Number 1 (Discussed during "Lesson 1 of Freedom from Mr Dolderer")

Cammy said that we'd need to find out what was "cool" at the moment so that we could get a better idea of what TNBT would be.

That's when I told her I was sure to the power of 1000 that we would probably be some of the last people in the school to find out what was cool and that by the time we had, it wouldn't even be cool any more. And that's when we realised that we didn't really want our band to be cool in a way that appealed to EVERYONE, and that we'd much rather be UNIQUE (which we're pretty good at) and have a small number of fans who really "got" our music. Cammy called them our "following".

Number 2 (Discussed during "Lesson 1.5 of Freedom from Mr Dolderer")

Once we'd decided that our band was going to be unique, it was time to decide what our musical style would be.

"I think we should probably figure out what instruments we're going to play first," I suggested. "You know, so we don't end up deciding to be a flute-playing rock and roll band."

But Cammy said that that was the EXACT OPPOSITE of what we should do (since we were trying to be unique) and that we should make the instruments "work for us" and not the other way around (whatever that means), and then she wrote down "Flute-Playing Rock Band", which made me laugh.

Then we decided that we should each write a list of our favourite bands and songs and then compare them to see the similarities.

It turned out there were SOME similarities, but those were mostly songs we both liked from when we were little. But what Cammy said she was much more interested in was what she called the "Key Difference" between our lists.

"You clearly prefer SLOWER songs," she explained. "I like really fast beats."

So to begin with we decided that our album would consist of five "slow" and five "fast" tracks. But then we had an even BETTER idea! We came up with the idea that WITHIN each song we would keep changing the speed from fast to slow; THAT would definitely be unique!

Number 3 (Discussed during "Lesson 2 of Freedom from Mr Dolderer")

Deciding which instruments we would each learn to play turned out to be the easiest and quickest Official Band Decision.

I went first and said that I'd always wanted to learn to play the keyboard, like my dad used to, and learn how to do all the awesome sound effects.

That's when Cammy said, "I support you in your decision to learn to play an unusual and unconventional instrument."

I didn't think the keyboard was very unusual or unconventional at all!

Then she said, "I hope you will be as supportive of me as I have been of your choice of instrument."

And that's when I knew she was going to say something BANANAS that stretched far beyond UNIQUE into "OH WOW" (in a bad way). So I prepared myself for her to declare that she had chosen to play the world's largest harp or one of those huge, vampire-ish organs with all the pipes that you get in churches. So when Cammy said she wanted to play the BONGO DRUMS I was very pleasantly surprised. The bongos are AWESOME!

More Official Band Decisions that were made in Chemistry class that week were:

- We needed a third band member to play the spoons, because we DEFINITELY wanted to be called "The Spoons" (to add to our "uniqueness").*
- I was going to use my dad's old keyboard and Cammy was going to make her own bongo drums using instructions she'd found on the Internet.
- As well as being "unique" we needed to come up with a USP (ASAP!)**
- We had to secure a venue for our first live performance.
- We had to start practising!

* I was not entirely convinced that having a spoon-player was the way to go, but agreed for the following reasons: (1) I liked the band name "The Spoons" (2) If I agreed to the spoon-playing I was allowed to say NO WAY to any other suggestion Cammy had – complete power! (3) I was 100% sure we wouldn't find a spoon-player at Fortress Academy.

** Cammy assured me that USP stands for "Unique Selling Point" and not a disease we'd learned about in Social Ed, as I had feared.

Once we'd decided we needed a third, spoon-playing, member for our band, Cammy wasted NO TIME AT ALL putting up a note on the Pupil Notice Board advertising this "Outstanding Opportunity". She even attached two REAL SPOONS to the note, to make sure it got attention (which it did).

By morning break that day, someone had ripped the spoons off the notice and written on it, "People Who Stick Spoons to Notices ARE spoons! GET A

LIFE! HA HA HA HA!" But even though our poster had been utterly defaced (probably by Year 10s, who seemed to live for this sort of thing) Cammy had a giant grin on her face.

And that's when I noticed (to my shock and slight horror!) that two of the little "tear-off" strips with the time, date and place of the spoon audition were gone.

That night, Cammy came over to my house so that we could start to write songs for our album.

Cammy said we should each sit in a MEDITATIVE

POSITION and let our current mood POUR OUT on to the page. And that WHATEVER came out we HAD to go with it – no changes. Because that way it would be more REAL.

And then Cammy said that that was exactly what her mum did when she was writing poetry, and all of a sudden I had this strange fear that Cammy's mum had maybe been one of the two people who had taken a little rip-off strip from our notice.

So anyway, I found us a writing pad each, and then sat down and started to write anything I could think of. I was trying my hardest to make it sound like the kind of stuff you maybe hear in a song, like "Today is the day of all the days", and "Stand up and show off your smiling hat" and all that. And to be honest, I felt like it was actually WORKING. I mean, I was probably in one of the best moods I'd been in since term had begun.

After a month at Fortress, things were eventually starting to "look-up", "improve" and even start to "be-much-less-horrific-than-the-beginning-of-the-term-when-Jessica-called-me-an-ugly-pigeon".

SPOON CRIME

As soon as I saw Cammy in registration the next day I knew something bad had happened. I'd already spotted two poopulars sniggering at the back of the room and Cammy looked as if she'd been crying.

"Cammy, what's wrong? Did they say something to you?" I asked as I sat down and gave one of the poopulars my best "go lick a snail" face.

"Nothing's wrong! Look at these!"

Cammy began eagerly showing me all of the songs she'd written when she'd gone home last night, and then she explained how some of them were so good that she'd been "moved to tears".

Then she pointed at me and said, "You've got

something on your shirt."

I looked down and saw the BIGGEST chocolate milk stain EVER.

The poopulars burst out laughing when Cammy began trying to rub it off with a tissue. That's when I realised it had been ME they'd been sniggering about earlier, not Cammy. And in that moment I cursed the curse of the Ugly Pigeon. But just then a boy I'd never seen before walked in and handed Mr Burton a note. And then he SMILED at me!

OK, so you're probably thinking, "Yeah, of COURSE he smiled at you – you looked like you'd been pooped on." But it wasn't like that. He wasn't smiling in THAT way, he was smiling in an ACTUALLY SMILING way.

Before I could even think about whether or not to ask Cammy if she knew who the boy was, Mr Burton told us that Year 7 had been called to attend an emergency assembly.

Everyone groaned and started getting up REALLY slowly, because we've been called to LOADS of these emergency assemblies so far this term (ALL of which have been about "crazes") and we've only been here for four weeks!

What usually happens is the head teacher stands on stage and warns us all not to take part in the latest craze, then demands that it "must end today or else!" But I really DO NOT understand why he does this, because clearly all the assembly does is actually SPREAD the craze even further.

I think the crazes are a "term one thing" where people who aren't as brilliantly unique as me and Cammy just want to copy whatever everyone else is doing so that they can fit in and avoid getting an Ugly Pigeon drawn on their locker.

When I told my mum about all the assemblies she said that the head is probably just trying to avoid a dangerous and violent "gang culture" starting in the school, which made me burst out laughing because one of the first (and most ridiculous) crazes was actually started by Cammy by mistake (and I can't really picture her as some sort of gang leader).

We were in the cafeteria and Cammy was half asleep because she'd been up all night mapping the planets and discussing alien life forms with her mum. *Anywayyyyyyyyy* … she was so tired that she kind of went all weird and started dipping her pizza in her milkshake (by mistake!). A few people must've spotted this and started copying Cammy and chatting about it because later that day we were all called to an emergency assembly.

The next thing you know, people started dipping all sorts of things: sandwiches, hot dogs, and I even saw one boy make a kind of meatloaf-float thing.

That's when the dinner ladies complained that we were all "animals", refused to serve us and went on strike, and we all got a letter home about "dipping".

One of the best crazes to have hit Fortress so far was "Eggy Language". This is where you take the first letter of a word, add the word "egg" to it and then attach the rest of the word. Let me "eggify" a sentence to show you what I mean:

Please stop using the metre sticks as swords.

This becomes:

Pegglease seggtop ueggsing tegghe meggetre seggticks aeggs seggwords.

It took a bit of practice to get right, but after about

a week we were all pretty fluent in Egg. In fact, Eggy Language got so big that it actually started to feel a bit weird when you tried to speak normally.

The teachers soon started to get REALLY annoyed at us. Mrs Rena, who teaches French, said that she could "NOT understand how we could have all more or less taught ourselves a foreign language in less than a week, but were still unable to master the simple basics of French after two years".

So that's when Bobby Hammer said, "That's because French is stupid." And got sent to the head's office.

To be fair, Bobby had a point. I mean, it doesn't matter how many times Mrs Rena tries to explain it to me, I DO NOT understand how a sofa can possibly be a "he" and a table a "she". I prefer my furniture to be genderless.

The major danger with crazes is that they can change mega-quick.

Like the time in Year 6 when wearing headbands became pretty much compulsory. And then swapping headbands became the new "wearing headbands".

Just about this time, I went on holiday during term-time because of a "family issue" that wasn't so much a "family issue" as it was a "holidays-are-cheaper-during-term-time-issue" and Mum just wrote a letter of lies and made me give it to my teacher. (Who then patted me on the shoulder and made a sad face.)

So anyway, we went to Spain on holiday and it was OK-ish.

Please see the following breakdown of events:

Good Points

I didn't have to go to school.

I didn't have to do Maths (well, actually that's not technically true, because at least forty times a day Mum would ask me, "How much is this in *real* money?" And I'd have to work it out for her.

I got a bit of a tan.

I touched a fish in the sea.

Bad Points

I had to share a room with Mum and Dad.

I was "force-friended" by my mum into spending every evening with an eight-year-old Welsh girl who was OBSESSED with horses and kept trying to get me to draws loads and give them names.

My parents drank WAY too much sangria and did

loads of embarrassing stuff, like laughing.

Mum sang on the karaoke (a lot).

I got burned on my left hand really badly and it grew to twice its normal size and stayed like that for the whole holiday. So every time Mum or Dad went to take a picture of me, I had to think fast and do something to hide my hand.

But the absolute BEST thing happened on the very last day.

I found this shop near the hotel that had these really cool headbands with elephants and parrots and geckos hand-painted on them. And they were HUGE.

So I got one for me and one for Cammy, and decided that maybe we should join in this "wearing/swapping headbands" thing but, you know, in a different, "gecko-dancing-with-a-leopard" kind of way.

So I turned up to school on Monday wearing my new awesome "arty" headband and noticed that people were staring at me. *Really* staring at me. I obviously assumed that the reason for this was because they were in AWE of my unique coolness, and that they were all itching to swap with me.

But when class started, Rachel Walker refused to sit next to me and had to be moved. I had no idea why. But then Cammy sent me a text from under her desk that said: LOSE THE HEADBAND ASAP. NITS OUTBREAK.

It turned out that while I was gone, all this headband-swapping had led to a serious head-lice epidemic.

Typical.

So for about two weeks after that everyone avoided me like the plague since I was the last one to be seen wearing a "Nit Band".

Note to reader: I am aware that I have been talking about crazes for a long time without actually telling you what THIS assembly was about. My apologies. I think I have been subconsciously trying to avoid thinking about what happened next.

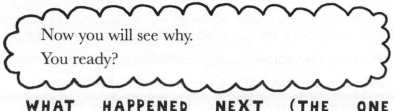

Now you will see why.

You ready?

WHAT HAPPENED NEXT (THE ONE MILLIONTH "EMERGENCY" ASSEMBLY)

This is when everything started to go wrong (band-wise).

The head teacher got up on stage and asked for silence. He then began explaining that crime (specifically THEFT) would not be tolerated at Fortress Academy.

I sat there wondering what had been stolen, assuming it must've been something quite serious, like someone's purse or one of the school laptops or something.

I was utterly and completely shocked when he said: "Stealing any form of utensil from the school cafeteria is a serious offence and will be dealt with *very* firmly indeed. I would hope that the person responsible for the recent theft will return the items before the end of day. Otherwise I will have no choice but to contact the authorities."

Cammy gripped my hand so tight I yelped.

LOADS of people turned round and stared at me.

Then the head teacher looked right at me and said, "Young lady, do you have something to say?"

And then EVERY SINGLE PERSON in the assembly turned round.

I felt my face burning. I wanted to turn and look at Cammy for help, but I literally couldn't move. I couldn't speak. I just sat there until the head teacher eventually said: "You are all dismissed. Except for you, young lady." He pointed at me. "I'd like a quick word with you in my office."

Then all of a sudden a prefect was escorting me to the head's office.

I sat outside and waited for the head teacher to call

me in. I actually had no idea what was going on. It had all happened so quickly!

There had clearly been some sort of misunderstanding. I hadn't stolen ANYTHING! Surely he would believe me? He might even laugh a little. Maybe he's not as stuffy as he seems when he's doing assemblies.

"Ms Perry, do come in."

Or maybe he is.

He made me sit there while he ignored me and talked to someone on the phone about paper for half an hour. By the time he put the phone down I wasn't really scared that I was in the head's office any more; I was bored. It felt like I'd been there FOREVER.

And then he started talking about the spoons. SPOONS! I couldn't help it, I actually burst out laughing when I realised that this was all about the two teaspoons Cammy had taped to our band notice. My God, this man seriously has WAY too much time on his hands. Spoon crime. That's what important to him. SPOON CRIME! Not finding some way to raise school funds so that pupils don't have to learn about Science from books that probably state the world is flat. No. Spoons. And paper, apparently.

"This is no laughing matter, Ms Perry," said the head.

For a second I was feeling so annoyed (and a bit brave) that I thought I might actually say how stupid I found this whole situation, and maybe even point out that he had WASTED over half an hour of my education by making me sit here while he FINALLY made a decision between thirty or forty ruled lines per page of A4 paper.

But I didn't. Obviously. I'm not THAT stupid.

Then he asked me if I'd taken the spoons. That's when I decide to take the blame. This man was clearly going to punish whoever had taken his precious spoons. And there was no way Cammy would survive prison (or a detention).

So I explain that I had BORROWED two teaspoons, and attached them to our notice, and that someone had then ripped them off and written all over it.

He looked at me blankly for ages, and then he said, "Is this a joke? Do you think you're being funny, Ms Perry?"

I was speechless.

He continued.

"Do you expect me to believe that a person would tape two spoons to a notice, let alone be advertising for a SPOON-player in the first place?"

To be fair to him, he had a point. It WAS a pretty unique thing to do (which was kind of the point).

"And what about the rest of the stolen spoons?" he asked.

My confused face must've said it all, because after that he stopped asking me questions and said:

"Fine. I would like you to go back to class now. But before you do, please be assured that I have my eye on you and this very *conveniently* named band of yours. Please collect a double detention slip from Mrs Segar on your way out. Good day."

And you know what? I just took the detention. It seemed like the easy way out of, well, whatever this was!

THE PHART
COLLECTION

LESSON – SOMETIMES YOU
HAVE TO BE CRUEL
TO BE KIND

Cammy had bitten off most of her nails by the time I got to Geography.

She listened intently as I explained about the weirdness of the head teacher, and about how he didn't seem to believe me when I told him about the notice and our need for a spoon-player, and also what he said about keeping an eye on our band.

I chose to leave out the bit about the detention because I didn't want Cammy to start crying again, or offering to dress up as me and go in my place. She already felt too guilty. "I can't believe you said it was you!" she said. "You could've been EXPELLED!"

"But I wasn't, OK? Just forget about it."

But Cammy would NEVER forget about it; she's sweet (and sometimes quite annoying) like that.

And then she reached over and gave me a hug.

"Thanks, Peri."

I thought about how I'd almost stood up to that crazy spoon-tyrant of a head teacher and saved my best friend, and it made me feel all, I don't know, hero-like, I suppose.

And then Mr Phart (yes, his name is Mr Phart. And yes, you say it like you say fart) started actually SHOUTING at us for chatting (he is an overreactor).

So that's when me and Cammy decided to silently protest against his shouty behaviour by finishing our work really quickly and then spending the rest of the lesson making the "Worst Subjects (with detailed justification) List". We both agreed that Geography should be at the top.

Please see the following reasons:

Reason 1: Geography involves Mr Phart.
Reason 2: He is OBSESSED with the Netherlands.
Reason 3: He wears sandals (with socks)

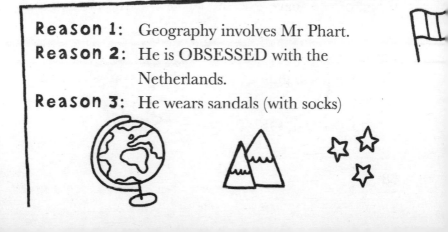

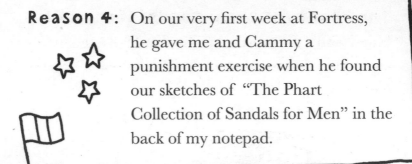

Reason 4: On our very first week at Fortress, he gave me and Cammy a punishment exercise when he found our sketches of "The Phart Collection of Sandals for Men" in the back of my notepad.

I was gutted when he ripped those sketches out. We'd worked really hard on them!

"The Phart collection"

The Phart Winter Sandal (for men):

This snazzy sandal has built-in snow grips and is finished in luxurious faux fur. Guaranteed to keep those hairy tootsies toasty during the cold winter months.

The Phart Air Blade Sandal (for men):

Fitted with a state-of-the-art Toe Fan™, these sandals are perfect for sweaty feet and bothersome cheese-toes.

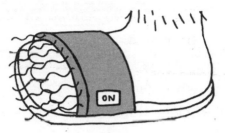

And my personal favourite:

The Luxury Limited Edition Phart Sandal (for men):

This super-sandal has specially designed built-in socks (one size fits all). Choose from the following fabulous colours: grey, greyer, greyest and off-white.

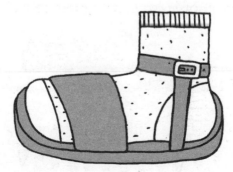

The day after Mr Phart found our sketches, he came to school wearing actual shoes.

He looked massively uncomfortable walking in them, like he'd never worn shoes in his life and wasn't quite sure what to do with them. They squeaked, which didn't help, and he kept shooting me and Cammy dirty looks, as if it was OUR fault HIS shoes were squeaking (which I suppose, to be fair, it was in a way).

I felt a bit guilty to begin with, but then I started to think about how we'd probably done him a favour. I mean, it's kind of like when I was eight and Mum threatened to sew my dummy to my school jumper if I didn't give it up once and for all (yes, I am well aware that eight years old is far too old to still be sucking a dummy). I knew that everyone would laugh at me if I turned up at school with it stuck to my jumper, so I surrendered my secret stash of dummies.

At the time, I remember thinking that Mum was just being really mean (especially since I knew for a fact that she had sucked her thumb until she was sixteen!). But now I realise that if she hadn't forced me to give it up, I might still be addicted to sucking a dummy today. Can you imagine? I'd have to be home-schooled!

So I suppose all the meanness was for my own good. Mum was only being cruel to be kind.

And even though Mr Phart might hate us just now, I'm sure he'll thank us for it one day. (Probably the day he eventually gets a girlfriend because he no longer wears socks and sandals.)

ONE OF THE WORST DECISIONS ANYONE HAS EVER MADE. EVER.

At the end of the day we sat on the grass beside the hockey field and waited for our first spoon-player to arrive.

It was probably a pretty stupid place to hold a spoon audition, since we were uncomfortably close to a lot of the poopulars, who had hockey practice, and also because the grass was wet.

Cammy had almost made us cancel the spoon audition because she was worried the head teacher might turn up and start asking more spoon-related questions. But I managed to talk her round.

But when the first spoon auditionee walked across the grass towards us I almost wished I HAD let

Cammy cancel. I couldn't breathe. And if it's possible, I'd actually forgotten how to keep my mouth in a normal position. I was panicking. I felt as though I had WAY too many teeth. And I was very aware of my tongue.

"Look!" said Cammy. "Someone's coming. It's a boy."

But it wasn't just "a boy". It was THE boy. It was SMILED-AT-ME BOY!

"Hey," said Smile Boy. And then he looked at me and SMILED AGAIN!

It was too much. I couldn't cope. I decided to be a statue.

"Are you here to audition?" Cammy asked, seemingly unaware of how amazing the boy was.

Smile Boy grinned and brought his hands out of his pockets. He had a spoon in each hand. Spoons suddenly seemed like the best things in the world.

It was at this point that I realised I hadn't been swallowing. Saliva had just been gathering in my mouth, and I was suddenly unsure about what to do with it.

Then Cammy said, "Whenever you're ready." And I thought she was talking to me, so I tried to swallow but it went down the wrong way (of course!) and I ended up having a very unflattering coughing fit and had to excuse myself and go inside to the toilets.

When I came back Smile Boy has morphed into the OPPOSITE of Smile Boy!

A redheaded girl stood slapping a pair of spoons on her thighs at rapid speed while Cammy clapped along vigorously.

"What's going on?! What happened to ... erm?"

I realised I didn't know Smile Boy's name.

It didn't matter. Nobody was listening to me anyway!

Cammy was now up on her feet dancing around the redheaded girl while she continued to play the spoons all over her body.

"Cammy! What happened to the boy that was here?"

"What? I can't hear you. Come and dance!"

"CAMMY! THE BOY! What happened?!"

"Oh! His audition didn't go well. He didn't make

the cut. But Cara's GREAT, isn't she?!"

OH.

MY.

GOD.

When Cara eventually finished her audition, Cammy didn't really give me a choice about whether or not we should ask her to join our band. In fact, I believe Cammy's exact words were:

"Cara, you're the BEST spoon-player I've ever heard, and there's no one left to audition, so ... Peri? What do you think? Can Cara join our band?"

I mean, what was the point of even asking me that? Just WHAT could I have said other than, "Yes"? (Which is exactly what I said, since Cara was standing RIGHT THERE.)

So anyway, I left them to chat spoons and headed home in a foul mood.

WHO IS THIS CARA PERSON??

The next day at school, Cammy said that it was time to plan our first official band practice. Despite the fact that I wasn't completely on board with Cara joining our band, I was really excited about our first practice.

We decided that lunchtimes and after school would be the best time to practise, since Cara had like a MILLION groups and clubs that she had to go to at the weekends.

However, we couldn't seem to find anywhere in school to practise.

Our music teacher, Mr Fry, was no help, and in fact seemed to hate us, our band and music in general.

Or at least that's the impression he gave us when we told him all about The Spoons and asked if there was anywhere we could play.

Rather than physically or even verbally applauding us for taking the initiative to form our own band (as a music teacher should) Mr Fry had looked personally insulted and told us that there were "no free music rooms whatsoever, at any time, on any day, especially at lunch or after school". Which was CLEARLY a lie because as soon as the bell rings at the end of the day, Mr Fry runs straight to his car, which means HIS room is free!

However, one of the other music teachers took pity on us. I thought her name was Miss Cardigan – although she doesn't look anything like a "Miss Cardigan" and looks more like a "Miss Zap" or "Miss Pop" or something like that, because she's really young, and always running around, organising loads of music stuff while Mr Fry just slumps at his desk drinking coffee.

Once Mr Fry had slammed his door and gone back to his desk, Miss Cardigan took us down to the very end of the music corridor, past all the old instruments and boxes, and said, "As long as you don't play too loudly, you're welcome to practise in here." And then she smiled, and I knew that her smile meant that we shouldn't let Mr Fry know.

We were MEGA-excited to have our own band space, and chose to ignore the fact that it was a large store cupboard with no windows and a weird smell. We didn't care – it was ours!

As soon as the bell went at the end of the day, I made Cara and Cammy wait while I made sure Mr Fry had driven out of the car park, and then we ran all the way to our practice cupboard.

When we went inside and pulled the light on I realised that not ALL the teachers at Fortress were a lost cause.

"Oh WOW!" said Cammy. "It looks like a professional recording studio!"

Cammy was exaggerating a bit, but it REALLY did look amazing!

Miss Cardigan had cleared out most of the old instruments and put in three chairs, a music stand … and an awesome new KEYBOARD!

Just then there was a little knock on the cupboard door, and Miss Cardigan poked her head in. "Do you like it?" she asked, grinning at us.

"We love it, Miss Cardigan!" I said. "Thanks so much for letting us borrow one of the new keyboards!"

"Well, I heard you talking about your instruments with Mr Fry, and didn't think you'd quite manage to lug a keyboard in here on your back every day for practice. You're welcome. Enjoy!" she said, before disappearing, and then reappearing a few seconds later. "By the way, it's Miss Carrigan," she giggled. "But I DO like cardigans – they match my pointy specs!"

Once Miss Carrigan had gone, we all chatted about how awesome she was and tried to guess what her favourite instrument might be. I thought she definitely seemed like someone who would play the electric guitar, but Cara said she thought she might play the flute, and Cammy agreed, which kind of annoyed me a bit.

"OK," said Cammy. "Let's get started. I have something to show you!"

And then she pulled the strangest pair of bongo drums I have ever seen out of her bag (not that I've seen a lot of bongo drums, but enough to know that these were weird).

"What do you think?" she asked, beaming proudly.

What I thought was that she'd used quite a few pairs of old tights to make the drum bit, and that she probably should've cut the long bobbly/holey leg bits off, which were hanging down like some sort of horrible drum-dress.

But what I said was, "Wow. Does it work?"

Cammy answered by giving me a drum solo. And it actually sounded great!

"The acoustics in here are perfect," she said, looking round the store cupboard.

Then Cara took a laptop out of her bag and put on a really fast dance track I'd never heard before. And then she produced her spoons and started playing along REALLY FAST. And it was (unbelievably) FANTASTIC!

"WOW!" I said (and meant it!). "That sounds amazing, Cara!"

Cara flicked her puffy red hair off her face and grinned. "OK, your turn!" Cammy squealed with excitement.

That's when I realised that I didn't really have anything to play for them, as I hadn't realised we'd all be expected to do brilliant solos today.

To be honest, I felt a bit stupid. I'd assumed that being the only one playing an instrument that wasn't home-made, or the spoons, I'd probably be the one carrying the band – you know, the best instrument/the leader/front-man. But having just heard how brilliant both Cammy and Cara were, I was feeling a bit nervous and awkward.

"Is it OK if I don't play right now? It's just, I need to get used to this keyboard. I've never played on it before," I lied. (I've played on it quite a few times in music class.)

"Of course, of course!" said Cara, who was still grinning from ear to ear.

So I put on the earphones and began composing my "brilliant" solo (no pressure!).

I tried to concentrate on what I was doing, but I couldn't help noticing how much Cammy was laughing at whatever Cara was saying. Was Cara funny? I hadn't expected her to be.

I realised that I still hadn't really spoken to Cara at this point, and didn't know much about her other than:

1 She played (and loved) the spoons (and was brilliant at playing them!).
2 She seemed to be in a LOT of clubs.
3 She seemed to really like Cammy.

Cammy, however, seemed to have got to know Cara quite well in less than twenty-four hours, and as we were packing up after practice I was a bit surprised to find out that they even seemed to have a couple of "in jokes".

That's when I decided I needed to make more of an effort to get to know Cara. I mean, even though it should've been Smile Boy playing the spoons in our band instead of her, Cara was a big part of my life now, since I'd decided that the band was a big part of my life.

"So, Cara, how did you start playing the spoons?" I asked.

"Um, I don't know," she said. "I just liked them."

"You're really good," I said. "Have you had lessons?"

"No," she said, avoiding eye contact with me.

She didn't really seem to want to talk to me. I decided to change the subject.

"What are you up to this weekend?" I asked.

"Erm. Nothing. Well, I'm busy. Sorry, um, I better go. I've got Spanish," she said, and then she rushed out.

"That was weird," I said.

"What was?" said Cammy.

"Cara!" I said.

"Was she?" said Cammy. I could tell she wasn't

really listening to me. She was busy trying to fix a hole in her bongos.

"Erm … yes!" I said. "I asked her what she was doing this weekend and she went all weird. She obviously didn't want to tell me."

"Of course she did!" said Cammy, suddenly paying full attention (probably because I'd said something negative about her New Best Friend).

"Cara's not like that. She's lovely!" she said, completely unaware of how rude Cara had just been to me (her *Actual* Best Friend).

So I decided just to drop it. Cammy wasn't getting it. Cara had definitely been weird. But I had no idea why.

PARENTS' EVENING:WHEN TWO WORLDS COLLIDE

LESSON — HIRE FAKE PARENTS AND TAKE THEM (IF YOU WANT TO SHOW YOUR FACE AT SCHOOL EVER AGAIN)

So even though everything was going brilliantly with our band (except for the weird Cara thing) even this brilliance could not begin to make up for the awfulness we were told about in registration that week.

The "Come and Get to Know Fortress" Term 1 Parents' Evening.

Parents' Evening is probably one of the worst things that has ever been invented. It's unnatural. I mean, your mum and dad meeting your *teachers*! What's all that about?

I always feel so weird when I see my mum in places where it is clearly against the rules of the universe for her to be seen:

Places my <u>mum</u> should **NEVER** be seen:

1 My <u>school</u>
2 My <u>bedroom</u> **!!!**
3 A changing room with *me* in it! (Mum has this weird "thing" where she <u>HAS</u> to come into the changing room with me when we're shopping for new clothes. And I have this "not-so-weird thing" where I don't let her)
4 Within a fifty-metre radius of anyone I know
5 Near anything "electronic"

ISSUES Associated with My Parents and Parents' Evening:

Mum: She's a "sharer".

Dad: Ignores all universally accepted social boundaries. I used to think he just didn't know what was "OK" and what wasn't. But recently I'm starting to think he knows fine well and is just *choosing* to ignore normal social protocol.

When I found out that Dad was working late that night I thought I'd hit the jackpot!

I was wrong.

To my horror, it turns out that Mum is even *less* inhibited when Dad's not around!

The first appointment went badly. I tried to stop her from saying things, but there wasn't really anything I could do. She was OUT OF CONTROL.

So I just had to sit there as Mum told embarrassing story after story (some about me, some about her) and listen as she clearly demonstrated that she has full-blown verbal diarrhoea.

You're probably thinking that I should have just stayed at home: a kind of "what-you-don't-know-can't-hurt-you" type of defence tactic. Perhaps. But I guess I felt more comfortable knowing just *how* embarrassed to be the next day (and for the rest of my life).

My second appointment was with Mr Phart. Unfortunately, things continued along the same dark path.

Mr Phart was in the middle of discussing my "inability to remember where any countries are" when I decided to leave for TWO MINUTES to go to the toilet. (Which I happen to know the *exact* location of because it actually MATTERS to my life.)

When I came back I found that the conversation

had taken a wrong turn.

Mum was telling Mr Phart all about how a man who looked exactly like Brad Pitt had once asked her to "run away with him" and how she and my dad weren't married at that time, and that it had taken all of her will to say no, because a man with shoulders like a rhino doesn't come along every day. And then she (very noticeably) started staring at Mr Phart's shoulders (which aren't at all rhino-like and are much more twig-like).

On the plus side, Mr Phart looked a bit scared of my mum after that, and he forgot to mention the sandal sketches AND my recent test score (which is a very good thing because my score was a very *bad* thing).

Cammy says that if Mr Phart ever gives me grief for not understanding what on earth "the Netherlands" are, then I should just say that my mum was asking after him, and that should do the trick.

Further low points of the evening:

Mum spent fifteen minutes telling my Computing teacher, Mr Harper, that he was "gorgeous" and should be on TV.

She told my PE teacher about my rash. And my new PE teacher happens to be quite young, and OK-looking I suppose, so that kind of made it all worse.

She told Miss Carrigan how she and my dad loved listening to classical music when they were spending "alone time" together. The conversation was starting to panic me (and make me feel violently sick) so I made the mistake of interrupting her. This interruption caused my mother to turn her attention towards me, and she then FOR SOME UNFATHOMABLE REASON started to tell Miss Carrigan all about the time I accidentally left for school without underwear and had to run home.

So when it was time to meet my Maths teacher, I suppose I just kind of gave up. Rather than staying by her side AT ALL TIMES in order to supervise her and make sure she didn't say anything COMPLETELY HUMILIATING (like that was working!), I decided just to leave her to it and go and hide in the library for a while.

After about half an hour of sitting with my head on the desk in a half-asleep state (I was way too

emotionally drained to read) I heard someone come in and walk towards me.

I looked up and saw Smile Boy and JESSICA CLARK making their way over to the computers.

Smile Boy smiled at me for an amazing THIRD time!

"Hi, Peri."

I felt as though I'd been shot in the throat. In a good way. Oh my God. Smile Boy knew my NAME!

Jessica said nothing. She just pretended I wasn't there and kept talking at Smile Boy and then she TOUCHED HIS ARM.

I was so shocked by the whole thing (and a bit groggy) that I didn't say a word. I just sat there like an idiot, gawking at them until they sat down at one of the computers. ONE of the computers, as in two seats pushed WAY too close in front of ONE computer.

I wasn't quite sure what to do next so I just kind of sat there for a minute before walking out (very quickly) to find Mum.

When I managed to locate my mother I was gutted to find that she was STILL sitting with my Maths teacher!

I sat down next to them. Mr Jackson turned his head slowly away from Mum and looked at me. He looked like he felt a bit sorry for me. And also a bit like he'd been crying. God only knows what she said to him.

So, after the whole "Mum-flirting-with-Mr Harper", Mum making my Maths teacher cry and Jessica touching Smile Boy's arm/sharing a computer thing, I didn't really think Parents' Evening could get much worse.

Note to the world: Never, EVER think this! I'm pretty sure that just *thinking* this is what actually causes things to get worse!

When we walked back to the assembly hall to sign out, Max Martin was on stage about to unveil one of his paintings as part of the "Let's Show Our Parents How Special We Are" show that some kids get forced into by their teachers.

At first I wasn't really sure what I was looking at. I think I was in shock. But then all the pieces of the painting started to come together. Like a horrible nightmare that you know you've had but you can't really remember until bit by bit it starts to come back to you.

Well, it was kind of like that, except this was real. And it was worse. And I'm pretty sure a little piece of me died.

Cammy was there, and she did one of those dramatic gasps that women do in old movies.

"No! Don't look!" she said.

But it was too late. I'd already looked. And I'd already seen the unicorns. And I'd already seen them frolicking in the swirly clouds. And I'd already seen that one of them had Max Martin's face. And that the other one had my face.

I couldn't believe it.

IT
WAS
HORRENDOUS!

I just kind of stood there for a bit. Frozen to the spot. I think I was hoping that if I didn't move, or even breathe, no one would realise it was me. But unfortunately for me (and for everyone else who has eyes), Max is really good at drawing faces.

So *everyone* knew it was unicorn-me.

And then it got worse.

Yes. It got worse.

"Peri, is that ... *YOU*?" It was Mum.

Oh God – I'd forgotten she was here.

"Let's go," I said as I tried to drag her towards the door.

But she was having NONE of it.

"It is, isn't it? That's YOU!"

And then I felt that all-too-familiar feeling of complete and utter PANIC. Like when you just *know* that your crazed lunatic of a mother is about to do something that will scar you for life, but it all happens so quickly that you don't really have time to defend yourself.

I seriously considered just starting to scream things like, "Who even *are* you?!" or "Help! This mad woman is trying to kidnap me!" But I didn't, because I knew I'd be grounded for life if I did. I also knew that I'd probably have to walk home if Mum got arrested (and it was raining).

Note to reader: I now wish I had screamed "Stranger Danger!" at the top of my lungs and watched as Mum was dragged away kicking and screaming by the police – being grounded for life would have been a small price to pay to avoid what happened next.

It went a bit like this:

"Fifty pounds!" Mum shouted at Max Martin.

I couldn't believe it.

"Mum! What are you doing?!"

Everyone went silent.

"SIXTY!" she shouted again.

Oh my God. She thinks this is some sort of AUCTION!

"ONE HUNDRED POUNDS!" she screamed.

Can I just point out here that NO ONE ELSE WAS BIDDING. My mother was just screaming amounts of money at Max Martin, who looked like he was going to cry.

"SOLD!" shouted Mrs Kelp, the Art teacher. "Thank you for your generous donation towards the school's Art Fund!"

And then she hurried on to the stage and snatched the painting off the stand.

At this point Max Martin actually *did* start crying, and ran behind the stage curtain.

But nobody seemed to notice.

Everyone was too busy staring at my mum as she ran up on to the stage to collect "IT".

And then Mrs Kelp started clapping really loudly at Mum. And after a while everyone else just kind of joined in.

And then Mrs Kelp HANDED MY MOTHER A MICROPHONE!

"Would you like to say a few words?"

Kill me. Kill me now.

Asking my mum if she'd like to say a few words into a microphone with a crowd of people watching her is like asking a naked tortoise if he'd care for a shell.

"Well, HELLOOOOOOO, *FORTRESSSSSSSS!*"

Nooooooo!

"My name is Maria Perry."

Noooooooooooooooooooooooooooooooooooo!

"And I just HAD to buy this absolutely *beautiful* painting of my daughter, Peri, and her boyfriend … erm, Max, is it?"

NOOOOOOOOOOOOOOOOOOOOOOOOOOOOO OOOOOOOOOOOOOOOOOOOOOOOOOOOOOO OOOOOOOOOOOOOOOOOOOOOOOOOOOOOO OOOOOOOOOOOOOOOOOOOOOOOOOOOOOO OOOOOOOOOOOOOOOOOOOOOOOOOOOOOO OOOOOOOOOOOOOOOOOOOOOOOOOOOOOO OOOOOOOOOOOOOOOOOOOOOOOOOOOOOO OOOOOOOOOOOOOOOOOOOOOOOOOOOOOO OOOOOOOOOOOOOOOOOOOOOOOOOOOOOO OOOOOOOOOOOOOOOOOOOOOOOOOOOOOO OOOOOOOOOOOOOOOOOOOOOOOOOOOOOO OOOOOOOOOOOOOOOOOOOOOOOOOOOOOO OOOOOOOOOOOOOOOOOOOOOOOOOOOOOO OOOOOOOOOOOOOOOOOOOOOOOOOOOOOO OOOOOOOOOOOOOOOOOOOOOOOOOOOOOO OOOOOOOOOOOOOOOOOOOOOOOOOOOOOO OOOOOOOOOOOOOOOOOOOOOOOOOOOOOO OOOOOOOOOOOOOOOOOOOOOOOOOOOOOO OOOOOOOOOOOOOOOOOOOOOOOOOOOOOO

OOOOOOOOOOOOOOOOOOOOOOOOOOOOOOOOOOO
OOOOOOOOOOOOOOOOOOOOOOOOOOOOOOOOO
OOOOOOOOOOOOOOOOOOOOOOOOOOOOOOOO
OOOOOOOOOOOOOOOOOOOOOOOOOOOOOOOO
OOOOOOOOOOOOOOOOOOOOOOOOOOOOOOOO
OOOOOOOOOOOOOOOOOOOOOOOOOOOOOO
OOOOOOOOOOOOOOOOOOOOOOOOOOOOOO
OOOOOOOOOOOOOOOOOOOOOOOOOOOOOO
OO!!!

I think I must've half blacked out after that. I remember seeing Cammy run for the sign-out sheet, and I guess she must've signed us out because the next thing I remember I was being dragged out of the hall by my hood.

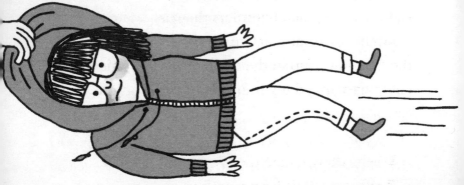

REALLY BAD ART CAN KILL

The next day I woke up to the sound of hammering. At first I thought I was still dreaming, because in my dream I had been sitting happily in class, sharing a seat and a computer with Smile Boy until an army of unicorns rushed in and began attacking me with those little wooden hammers they use at auctions.

I went downstairs (at 6am!) to find my mum hanging the "painting" up in the dining room. At this point I could have asked my mum a million questions. Such as:

1 Why do you hate me?
2 What *exactly* is wrong with you?

3 Just *who* is going to be able keep their food down with THAT thing staring back at them?

But I didn't say anything. I just did not have the strength to "engage" with my mother at 6am. So I just stood at the fridge and had five spoons of peanut butter (for energy) and then decided to get ready and go and see Cammy before school.

Cammy opened the door in her pyjamas.

"Hi?" she kind of asked. "You OK?"

What kind of question was that to ask me? Had she somehow *erased* the horror that was last night from her brain?!

"No. Let me in. I need to see Margaret."

I needed advice.

"You can't."

"What? I can't come *in*?"

"No, of course you can come in. It's just … there's something wrong with Margaret."

"Is she OK?"

Cammy looked like she was going to start crying.

"I don't know. Mum's about to take her to the emergency vet now."

Just then Cammy's mum appeared at the door with Margaret in her cat carrier. Margaret looked terrible. So did Cammy's mum.

"Hello, Peri, in you come."

Then she added, "Make sure Cammy remembers to eat her seeds before you leave," as she hurried Margaret into the car.

So we went up to Cammy's room, and that's when she told me what had happened to Margaret.

Note to reader: In order for you to understand the significance of what Cammy told me next, I'll need to tell you more about Margaret.

Margaret is no ordinary cat. Now, I know people maybe say that a lot. But listen to me when I say:

MARGARET IS NO ORDINARY CAT!

♡   ♡   ♡   ♡   ♡   ♡

MARGARET

Margaret is Cammy's cat. She is a very wise cat.

Cammy and I first noticed that Margaret was "special" when we were rummaging around in her big sister Meg's room (real name Nutmeg) looking for something to dye our legs with.

Background information relating to why we would want to dye our legs

Cammy had convinced me that the way to avoid that horrible yucky feeling you get when you have to put your tights back on in the sticky warm changing room after you've been swimming was to dye our legs black, grey or red (since these were the only colours accepted at our school). We were only eight at the time.

So, as I was saying, we were rummaging around in the bottom of Meg's wardrobe (which Meg would actually KILL US for doing if she ever caught us) when Margaret started making a weird screechy sound, and her ears began twitching like mad.

So Cammy asked Margaret if she was OK, and Margaret's eyes went really big and her right ear went completely flat. And then for some strange reason we just KNEW that Margaret was trying to tell us something.

Something *important*.

"I think we should get out of here," said Cammy. "I feel weird."

And I felt a bit weird too because Margaret was freaking me out. So we put everything back as quick as we could and ran out. And JUST as we got out of there and into the hall, Meg came out of the bathroom! She had her head all wrapped up in a towel and a bit of mousy-brown hair was hanging out the side.

"Hello, Nutmeg," I said.

I don't know why. I panicked.

Meg stared at me.

"When did you get back?" said Cammy. "You're

meant to be staying with Dad all weekend!"

"Was," said Meg. "New girlfriend kept laughing at my hair."

"So you've dyed it brown," I said.

SHUT UP, PERI! I swear I'm getting my mum's "talking" disease.

Meg just stared at me without blinking.

"Mum will probably cry," said Cammy. "It took her ages to get your hair that blue."

And then I pulled Cammy into her bedroom and shut the door because I didn't like the look in Meg's eyes. It's like my dad says when my mum's in a RAGE about something. Do NOT poke the wild beast!

So anyway, that's when we realised that Margaret had saved us. Margaret had somehow psychically KNOWN Meg was about to catch us in her room and warned us to prevent our deaths.

I love Margaret.

So, once Cammy's mum and Margaret had left for the emergency vet, Cammy told me what had happened to Margaret. She said that when she'd got home from Parents' Evening the night before, she'd found Margaret sitting on the dining table with her ears completely flat and that she was just STARING at the wall, and not really moving.

Then Cammy said that at bedtime she couldn't get Margaret to come to bed, which was even *weirder* because Margaret ALWAYS goes to bed when Cammy goes to bed, because she likes to sleep on Cammy's feet.

Cammy said that she'd set her alarm to go off every two hours so she could get up and check on Margaret. But every time she got up to check, Margaret was still just sitting there *staring* at the wall. And then at 6am Cammy said she heard Margaret SCREAMING and ran downstairs to find Margaret was CRAZED and furiously ripping all the wallpaper off the wall at the same spot she'd been staring at all night!

And that's when I realised what had happened. MARGARET KNEW ABOUT THE PAINTING! She'd had a premonition! So I told Cammy all about how I'd been woken up at EXACTLY 6am because of all the hammering and that

Mum had been hanging the unicorn painting on the DINING ROOM WALL!

I felt *terrible*! The hideousness of Max's painting had tormented Margaret to the point of madness. Poor Margaret.

Once I'd finished explaining what had happened to Margaret, Cammy grabbed her coat and put it on over her pyjamas.

"Come on!" she yelled, and started running down the stairs.

"Wait! Where are you *going*?!"

"WE NEED TO DESTROY THE UNICORNS BEFORE THEY KILL MARGARET!"

OPERATION UNICORN MASSACRE

LESSON — SOMETIMES YOU HAVE TO LIE IF A CAT'S LIFE IS AT STAKE

By the time we got back to my house it was still only 7am, and Mum hadn't left for work yet. I didn't have a CLUE what we were going to do, or how I was going to explain why Cammy was in her pyjamas, or why she looked like a madwoman (and also why she was probably going to set fire to Mum's painting!).

But as it turned out, I didn't have to. Mum didn't even seem to notice we were there. She was too busy being in a "mood". And then I noticed that the painting was gone.

I asked Dad about it (Mum looked a bit too "dangerous" to be asking her any questions) and he said that he had taken it down because he couldn't face eating his prunes with the "unicorn-fiasco" staring at him.

But wait.

Don't celebrate for me yet.

Can you guess where my dear mother decided to put it?

Of course.

Where else?

The painting looked even bigger in my tiny room. I shut the door and looked at Cammy with my serious eyes.

"Cammy," I whispered. "No one can ever know."

Cammy nodded.

"We have to make this look like an *accident*, OK?"

Cammy nodded again.

And that's when we came up with our brilliant plan:

Operation Accidentally-On-Purpose

Destroy Sick Painting and Save

Margaret's Life

Step 1: Find painting-destroying materials (blackcurrant juice, blue nail varnish, Mum's hair dye, scissors).

Step 2: <u>Attack</u> painting.

Step 3: <u>Strategically</u> place all empty containers and scissors on ground below painting.

Step 4: Place large *Oxford Dictionary* by door.

Step 4: Overturn chair and desk.

Step 5: Both lie on floor and scream, "OUCH! OUR LEGS. <u>PLEASE HELP!</u>"

The plan went down like this:

"OUCH! OUR LEGS. PLEASE HELP!"

Enter Mum.

"Oh my God! Are you all ri—"

Mum spots the painting (which was now a

"unicorn-massacre").

"MY PAINTING!!"

"My LEG!" I scream. (For real this time! Mum stood on me by mistake while rushing towards her "beloved" painting.)

"We tripped over the large *Oxford Dictionary*," said Cammy.

"And then we fell into the desk and the chair and spilled all of these containers," I said.

"And then the scissors flew up and opened mid-air," Cammy added.

Mum didn't look convinced.

I had to think fast.

There was a tiny scratch on my leg from where Mum's high heel had nicked me.

I squeezed it and squeezed it.

I am a genius.

"I'm hurt, Mum, look!"

"STEVE, GET UP HERE NOW! IT'S AN EMERGENCY!"

It turns out that the "emergency" Mum was referring to was 2% my injured leg and 98% the "unicorn-massacre".

Mum made Dad phone all the painting restorers he could find online, even though I'm pretty sure that even a painting restorer with actual magical powers wouldn't be able to fix what me and Cammy had done.

But it was all worth it. Because a few minutes later Cammy's mum sent Cammy a text to say that the vet had given Margaret the all-clear.

PERI & CAMMY'S MEGA JAM SESH!

The next few days were hell. EVERYONE at school thought Max Martin was my boyfriend, INCLUDING SMILE BOY. It was a disaster.

The difficult thing about an incorrect rumour is that people tend to talk about it behind your back; hardly anyone actually comes up and asks you if it's true or not. They mostly just accept that it's true, especially if they want it to be. There's very little you can do about it other than wait it out and hope that some poor person is accused of eating chips out of a bin or something, which then takes the heat off you.

At one point in the school cafeteria that week, I witnessed two poopulars walk up and say something to Max, to which he responded with a little smile and shy little shrug.

The poopulars in question then looked at me and began giggling. I almost lost it there and then. I actually had to hand my plate of pasta back to the dinner lady (which she was FURIOUS about) because I knew that if I didn't leave the cafeteria right away I'd definitely scream:

"MAX MARTIN IS NOT, AND NEVER WILL BE, MY BOYFRIEND!"

But I knew that as much as that would get the truth "out there", it would also put ME further "out there" and I'd probably end up being laughed at even MORE.

Cammy threw her egg sandwich back into the fridge and ran after me all the way to the music cupboard.

She said that even though today wasn't a "scheduled rehearsal" we should still definitely "jam" to help me get my "feelings" out. So we did.

I'm not sure if it was because it was just me and Cammy, or if it was due to my raging anger, but I suddenly didn't feel bothered about playing random things in front of Cammy without rehearsing them first, so I unplugged the headphones and just went for it!

Cammy went mad on the bongos, and every sound effect I hit on the keyboard seemed to blend PERFECTLY. We even managed to make up a crazy-good, half-fast/half-slow song that had us both in hysterics. We were going bananas, and at one point Cammy was lying flat out on the ground with her eyes closed and I'd put on Cammy's glasses and both of our jackets. I don't know why. But it was HILARIOUS!

If other people had been able to hear our music, they probably would've thought that we'd gone mad, especially at the bit where the only sound effect that fit with Cammy's percussion (in my mind) was the noise of a dog barking repeatedly for almost a full minute. But we thought it sounded great!

Me and Cammy laughed MUCH more than she had with Cara during our first band practice. It was awesome, and definitely the best fun I'd had in months!

MARGARET'S SECRET

LESSON — BE VERY NICE TO YOUR CAT. YOU NEVER KNOW WHO THEY MIGHT HAVE BEEN IN A PREVIOUS LIFE.

The day after our "mega jam sesh", we arranged with Cara to have a band meeting at Cammy's that night. It was going to be our most important band meeting yet.

Cammy had typed up an agenda and asked us to keep the whole night free.

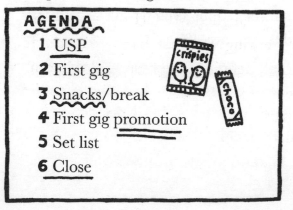

AGENDA
1 USP
2 First gig
3 Snacks/break
4 First gig promotion
5 Set list
6 Close

I REALLY wanted to say that there was quite a lot on the agenda and to suggest that we have the meeting at the weekend, because I knew that Cara wouldn't be able to come (since she'd made it clear she was "busy").

I'd decided that one of two things was going on with Cara: (1) She was hiding something that she didn't want us to know, or (2) She just didn't like me.

Either way, I would have much rather she wasn't at the meeting. That way I could just relax, and me and Cammy could have fun like we'd had the day before – like we ALWAYS used to before starting at Fortress.

But then (quite suspiciously) Cara turned up at Cammy's and said that she couldn't stay. She said she had some sort of emergency group/club/committee meeting thing. But I didn't really believe her because she wouldn't look me or Cammy in the eye when she said it. And then she rushed out and got back in her mum's car and they drove off.

I thought about bringing up the whole "I-told-you-Cara-was-being-weird-and-now-I-definitely-think-she's-hiding-something" thing, but I decided just to leave it and enjoy myself.

So me and Cammy made a "Band-Snack-Plate"

and began discussing the agenda.

Agenda Item 1 - USP

It was actually kind of spectacularly, amazingly spooky and perfect how we came up with our Unique Selling Point. We were mid-jam when we both noticed that Margaret was STARING at us from the seat Cammy had put out for Cara.

And then all of a sudden she started wailing and making all sorts of weird noises and we both just instantly KNEW that Margaret:

a wanted to be part of our band
B was awesome
C was going to be our Unique Selling Point!!! (And clearly, having a cat in your band is the most awesomely amazing band USP ever, ever, EVER!!)

We kept playing, and trying loads of new stuff. Margaret was absolutely LOVING it. At one point Meg came in and accused us of bothering Margaret, though she didn't put it that nicely. But when she tried to take Margaret away from our "hideous noise" Margaret flopped out and made her body all heavy, which is what she does when she wants to stay somewhere. So Meg left in an even worse mood than when she came in.

And that's when Cammy said, "Oh my God. Do you think Margaret was maybe a singer in a band or something in a previous life?"

So I played a little tune on the keyboard and looked at Margaret and she looked WAY happy. And then Cammy did the same on the bongos and Margaret made a BRILLIANT sound.

"What if she's the reincarnation of a rock-god or something?" I said.

We were excited by this idea and decided to try to find out WHO Margaret had been in a previous life by playing her songs by loads of dead rock-gods.

So we went online and played tune after tune to Margaret until eventually her ears went completely flat and her body did that still thing and she opened her eyes wider than I've ever seen her open her eyes before (or that I knew was even possible). And that's when we KNEW she was the cat reincarnation of Elvis.

We started making plans immediately:

1 Margaret would sit on a podium and ad-lib throughout the performance.

2 Margaret would be the face of The Spoons – we'd make up T-shirts and badges, and put her on the front of our album.

3 We would prepare ourselves for STARDOM!

RARE ARM HAIR FOR SALE

LESSON — I HAVE NO IDEA. SOMETIMES MY LIFE IS JUST TOO WEIRD.

The only problem we had in relation to creating lots of band merchandise (spectacularly decorated with Margaret's face surrounded by spoons) was that we didn't have ANY money to pay for the flyers, badges, T-shirts, wristbands and Margaret-mugs. We'd used our savings on Cammy's criminal name-change.

We were planning to ask Cara if she could chip in when we saw her at lunch practice that day, but she ended up having to cancel again because of one of her clubs.

(I was starting to wonder just how committed Cara WAS to The Spoons, since she'd missed the big meeting at Cammy's and then another band practice.)

So we had the BEST, most UNIQUE band EVER, but no money to successfully promote ourselves.

However, sometimes life can surprise (and disgust) you in equal measure.

It happened after lunch when I opened my workbook in Maths and found one of Mr Jackson's arm hairs between the pages. I knew it belonged to Mr Jackson because he's got quite hairy arms, and I'm guessing he would have been using them in the process of marking my workbook.

So anyway, I nudged Cammy and pointed to the hair, and she said that she thought we should keep it.

"What? Why?!" I said. "That's gross!"

"No, it's fine. We can sell it!" she said. And then she picked it up and put it in her sandwich bag (with her crusts). It was disgusting.

I had no idea who would possibly want to purchase one of Mr Jackson's gross arm hairs (currently nestled in smoked-salmon sandwich crusts), but Cammy was adamant that loads of girls at Fortress *loved* Mr Jackson. Cammy said she was pretty sure that if she could "authenticate" the hair, then she could sell it or

123

trade it for something big.

I did not agree (unless by "big" she meant an even longer hair).

But (scarily) it turned out that I was wrong.

Word of the captured arm hair spread throughout the school. Some of the girls in the year above even came up to us and asked to see it! But Cammy said that there was to be no viewing until tomorrow, once the hair had been properly "prepared".

So that night I reluctantly went round to Cammy's house to help her "prepare" the hair for the sale. We got an old ring box, and placed the hair gently on the white cushion, and closed the lid. After that, I

thought we were done (especially since we'd risked our lives by sneaking into Meg's room and stealing a ring box) but Cammy said we still needed to create the "Authentication Document".

So Cammy spent *ages* making this really official-looking document on her computer, which said things like:

I hereby declare that The Hair is truthfully and lawfully a former resident of Mr T. Jackson's forearm (unable to certify if right/left).

Then she said that I was the one who had to sign it (since I had discovered "The Hair").

I did not want to sign this document for the following (obvious) reasons:

Obvious Reason 1
I would look completely mad.
Obvious Reason 2
YUCK!
Obvious Reason 3
Cammy's document looks so official (and had the tiniest "small print" I have ever seen) that I was scared that if I signed it I might actually be entering into a marriage with The Hair.

To cut a long story short, she forced me to do it. Cammy is a very convincing person.

At least I know that if I ever do anything wrong when I'm older, like accidentally murder my parents, Cammy will be able to convince the judge that *I* am, in fact, the victim.

The next day we had a very successful viewing session (except for the part where a sad-looking girl in the year above drooled on my hand a bit when she was reading the Authentication Document).

In the end, Cammy took a surprise phone call and then said that the sale had gone "private" and that the buyer had asked to remain anonymous as part of the agreed sale. When I asked how much we had sold the hair for, all Cammy said she could tell me was that it had been sold for a "significant amount" and that she wouldn't be able to tell me until the sale had "finalised" (whatever that meant). However, I was assured that I would receive 50% of the profit, so I wasn't really bothered. I mean, if I'd been sad enough to purchase a human arm hair, I'd want to remain anonymous too!

SOCKS
SUCK

A few days later we EVENTUALLY managed to meet with Cara to update her on all the new band stuff.

"I'm sorry I've not been able to come to rehearsals," said Cara when we got to the music cupboard.

"That's OK," said Cammy. "Is everything all right?"

"Oh yes!" said Cara. "I've just had to help my mum, you know, erm, go to the dentist and stuff. She's really scared of the dentist."

Cammy nodded that she understood, and began telling a story about her worst dentist experience.

I couldn't believe it! No WAY was Cara telling the

truth. How many times did her mum have to go to the dentist?! And what type of dentist is open after seven on a Friday night?

That's when I remembered that Cara had said she had some sort of emergency committee meeting or something when she'd turned up at our planning meeting and then left.

"How was your committee meeting?" I asked.

"Oh. That. It was cancelled," she mumbled, and then she started playing her spoons really loud (obviously so I couldn't ask her any more questions).

She was definitely hiding something.

After practice, Cammy told Cara all about Margaret and our awesome plans.

Cara thought that having Margaret as a fourth band member was "inspired" and immediately began composing a spoon-percussion beat in Margaret's honour.

Cammy said that she'd had to make a few "executive decisions" when ordering the band merchandise online with her mum last night, and that she'd managed to get some T-shirts and a few mugs. But that instead of the badges and wristbands, she'd seen an "unbelievable offer" for personalised

socks, so she'd spent most of the money from the arm-hair sale on those.

I was furious. I mean, we'd spent AGES together at the weekend deciding EXACTLY what to buy, and how many, and how much, etc, etc. And  Cammy had just gone and changed everything without even talking to me about it!

"We can't go round the school giving out SOCKS!" I blurted out (in not a very nice way) before I could stop myself.

Cammy looked shocked.

"I thought you'd like them," she said. "They're much more unique than badges or wristbands, aren't they?"

"I think socks are a great idea," said Cara.

Of course she did. She thinks EVERYTHING Cammy does is brilliant.

So I just shut up about the socks, and said that everything was fine even though it wasn't. But there wasn't really anything I could do about it.

The rest of the practice went OK. We chatted a bit about Margaret, and Cara managed to learn all the new songs we'd written at the weekend really quickly.

We got so caught up in everything that we didn't actually hear the end-of-lunch bell, and ended up having to drop everything and literally RUN to class.

That night Cammy sent me an SOS text:

> **MY ROOM. 7.30PM. MEETING OF MAJOR IMPORTANCE. BE THERE. BRING YOGHURT.**

I knew this was going to be bad. When everyone else freaks out and eats a gallon of peanut-butter-chocolate-chip-cookie-dough ice cream, Cammy has a sugar-free yoghurt.

Thankfully, Cammy just lives around the corner, so I was able to get there quickly since this was obviously an emergency.

When I arrived, Margaret was already waiting on her cushion. She looked wise.

Cammy did not look wise. She looked unhinged.

"I think we need to do something *crazy*," she said

(with a serious face). "Something that will make the whole school notice us."

I just looked at her.

"Why would we do that?" I said.

Cammy jumped up and looked me straight in the eye.

She was so close I *swear* our eyeballs were almost touching.

"Because we need to find our FOLLOWING, Peri!" she said. "How are we going to find our following and get them to our first gig, if nobody even knows we exist?"

It seemed like a good point so I sat down, took a yoghurt and listened to Cammy's "brilliant idea".

I cannot even begin to tell you how much I wish I had done a double forward roll across the room, back-flipped out of the window and sprinted all the way home before she could open her crazy mouth.

Please see the following chapter (and maybe have a biscuit handy for when it gets *really* bad).

WELCOME TO THE WORST IDEA IN THE WORLD

The introduction of "The Worst Idea in the World™" went a bit like this:

"Peri, what's the ONE thing we could do in the cafeteria that would DEFINITELY make people notice us?"

I have paid *just* enough attention in Mr Rhubarb's English class to know that what Cammy is asking me is a "rhetorical question".

I answer anyway.

"Eat our own arms?"

Cammy gives me a "look".

"No. We're going to do a 'flash-mob dance'! This will get everyone's attention and introduce a flavour of The Spoons to the cafeteria. Peri, just imagine everyone's reaction when one minute you, me and Cara are standing in line and then the next minute we're dancing for everyone to see!"

"HA HA HA HA HA HA HA!"

"Now, watch me. I've choreographed a routine. Some of the high-kicks are a bit tricky, but I think—"

"Wait, you're not serious?"

"Of course I am. It's perfect!"

"Only if perfect means completely *horrific*! Cammy, this is a BAD idea. Flash-mobs are usually, well, MOBS! Loads of people. People who can actually DANCE!"

But Cammy wasn't listening.

She was too busy trying to do the splits.

And that's when I started to get scared. I mean, even though I knew that there was NO WAY IN THE WORLD I was going to be part of a three-person flash-mob, I still felt a bit nervous, you know, like when you make eye contact with a police officer, and you know you've done absolutely nothing wrong, but you still start to get a bit nervous "just in case".

There was only one solution. I was determined not to use my one-and-only "no way" vote unless I absolutely HAD to, especially since Cammy's bad ideas seemed to be getting worse (first the socks; now this!). I wondered if this was Cara's influence.

I knew that we'd have to ask Margaret. Margaret was now the only one that could stop Cammy from plunging herself (and me!!) head-first into the Worst Idea in the World. I mean, I'm SURE dancing in the cafeteria would get our band noticed. And YES, I'm all for "uniqueness"…

HOWEVER…

there's a line. I do not wish to be one of "those kids" who get slices of ham thrown at them in the cafeteria. And I'm pretty sure doing a so-sad-it-makes-butterflies-cry dance in front of the WHOLE SCHOOL would definitely lead to sandwich filling being thrown in our general direction. It's one thing to be a bit "different", but it's a completely *other* thing to be INSANE.

I looked at Margaret. She was sitting like a hen. This was a very good thing. Margaret always seems at her wisest when she's like that.

So Cammy agreed to ask for Margaret's opinion.

"Margaret," I said softly. "You are looking very beautiful today."

"Stop it!" said Cammy. "Just ask her."

"Fine. Margaret, do you think we should completely humiliate ourselves in front of the *entire school* by doing a three-person flash-mob dance in the cafeteria tomorrow?"

Margaret stared at me and then looked out of the window for a bit.

"She's not interested," I said. "That means no."

"No it doesn't," said Cammy. "Just give her a minute. She's thinking."

Margaret continued to stare out of the window.

"Come on, Cammy. It clearly says in 'The Book' that if she shows a 'notable lack of interest' then the question has bored her whiskers off, and is therefore NOT a good idea."

"It doesn't say that, Peri."

"Um ... I think you'll find it does, *Cammy.*"

"Oh really? I think you'll find it doesn't, *Peri!*"

"OK, let's look then, shall we?" I said.

So Cammy went and got "The Book".

Note to reader: "The Book" is made up of a list of all of the noises/movements Margaret makes when she's trying to tell us something and their carefully decoded meanings.

Over the years, Cammy and I have managed to figure out what Margaret is trying to tell us (most of the time) through analysing her various sounds and movements.

We've actually started to do some of them ourselves, to warn each other of impending DANGER.

Like the time in biology, when Cammy was hiding worms in her gym bag because we knew the boys

were going to torture them next lesson with the acid (rather than just putting it near them and observing their behaviour, like Mr Herbert had said to do).

But then Mr Herbert spotted that Cammy was up to something and started to make his way over to her, so I started "chattering" really loudly to warn her.

Background information: "Chattering" is a really weird noise that Margaret makes sometimes. It sounds a bit like a mix between a bird and a machine gun (if you can imagine that). It kind of sounds like "EEERER ERER RERERERERERERERERE". Cammy and I give chattering a serious score of 9 on the "Margaret Warning Scale".

So anyway, Cammy got the warning and managed to slip the last of the worms into her bag without being caught. And then Mr Herbert sent me to the school nurse (I'm not exactly sure why, but I went anyway because I was a bit bored).

Unfortunately for the "rescued" worms, Cammy's dad picked her up by surprise after school and took her out for tea. When she got home she realised she had forgotten all about the worms, and that most of them were squished.

SO … Cammy went to get "The Book", but before we could even look at it, Margaret starting making a weird *low* sound. It was freaky. It sounded like it was coming from really deep inside her. Like from her tail or something. We'd never heard her do that one before. It was *definitely* new.

"I think that's a very clear NO," I said firmly.

Cammy nodded slowly and I was mammothly relieved.

IS THIS REAL LIFE??

LESSON — NEVER LET YOURSELF BE BLINDSIDED BY THE WORST IDEA IN THE WORLD

Cammy was acting really weird at lunch the next day. She had her coat zipped right up, and she was wearing a scarf even though it was boiling in the cafeteria.

"Are you still upset that Margaret didn't like your idea?" I asked her.

"No," said Cammy matter-of-factly. "Because Margaret didn't actually say that."

And then I had a horrible sinking feeling.

Oh God.

Something was about to happen.

Before I could get out of there, Cammy blindsided me at the baked-potato station and ripped her coat off to reveal a sort of half-peacock/half-mermaid leotard thing. At this point (even though I was 99% certain I'd dressed myself this morning) I started to panic that *I* had one on underneath my coat too!

Everything got even weirder after that.

As soon as Cammy's coat hit the floor, she started kicking her legs and headbutting the air. And then she started pointing at me!

First she did it with her left arm, then with her right,

and then it kind of became part of her "dance". And that's when I realised there was music playing really quietly (it was coming from Cammy's phone).

I had to make a choice. And there wasn't much time. I either just stood there and let my best friend humiliate herself in front of the entire school, or I did what a best friend should do and go down in flames with her.

To be honest with you, I hadn't really made up my mind when Cammy grabbed me by the arms and started pulling me back and forth, and spinning me around.

But then her phone fell out of her leotard pouch and hit the ground. And the music stopped. And so did our "dance".

And it turns out Cammy was absolutely right. We had the full attention of EVERYONE IN THE ENTIRE CAFETERIA (just NOT in a good way).

IN HIDING

LESSON — SMILES CAN BE DECEIVING

I was supposed to meet Cammy and Cara after school that day for band practice, but I had to make up an excuse so I could go to detention for stealing the spoons that I didn't steal.

To be perfectly honest, I wasn't that bothered about not going to practice. Cammy had completely humiliated us in the cafeteria that day, and I didn't really feel like being around her just then in case she came up with another "brilliant idea" to promote our band.

Cara had proved to be no help when I'd tried to explain to Cammy how embarrassing the cafeteria incident had been. And when I suggested that we

NEVER do anything like that again and that we hand out flyers instead, Cara actually disagreed with me and told Cammy that she thought her flash-mob had been the perfect "eco-friendly" way to "raise awareness" of our band. And then Cara made me want to stuff her mouth full of memorabilia socks when she suggested to Cammy that we plan another flash-mob!!

So anyway, I left them to practise and plot my future embarrassment by themselves, and said that I had to go and get my hair cut. I almost told Cammy I was off to do HER detention but I managed to stop myself. Yes, I was annoyed at Cammy for not listening to me about the terrible dance, but I didn't want to make the whole situation worse.

When I arrived at detention, I instantly regretted admitting to the "spoon theft".

As I looked round the room I spotted at least four poopulars, one of whom was Jessica Clark.

"Peri!" said Mrs Kelp, clearly surprised to see me there.

She scanned the register. "You have a double detention?" She sounded almost sorry for me. I nodded. "Please take a seat. There's paper and a pen on the desk."

I sat there in silence, surrounded by poopulars, and thought about how unbelievably stupid I'd been. I knew that I should've just told Cammy about the detention rather than lying to her about going to get my hair cut. Cammy HATES lies. But the only reason I'd lied, and the only reason I was there, was because I was trying to be a good friend. And now I had to go home and cut my own hair.

But then I started to think that maybe I WOULDN'T cut my own hair. I mean, why should I always be the one trying to be a good friend? It wasn't as though Cammy was exactly being a good friend by humiliating me in the middle of the school cafeteria, banishing gorgeous spoon-players from our band and being obsessed with Cara!

I stared at the blank paper. There was no instruction sheet, and nothing written on the board. I assumed we were free to write what we wanted, and began to channel my angry mood into a song called "Why Did You Have to Banish the Gorgeous Spoon Player, Cammy? Why?" And I was REALLY getting into it when Mrs Kelp said, "Ah. You decided to join us. Do have a seat."

I was determined not to stop writing while I was in "the zone" but was forced to look up when a voice said, "Do you mind if I sit here?"

It was Smile Boy!

He sat down next to me.

"What are you writing?" he whispered.

I remembered how to use my arms just in time and threw them across the paper so he wouldn't see. It was a bit over the top.

"Wow. Something private, I guess. Sorry," he whispered, and smiled at me again.

"Edward!" called Mrs Kelp.

Smile Boy raised both hands, as if to say sorry, and began writing.

His name was Edward. My heart was beating so loud I was convinced other people could hear it too.

I sat there staring at what I'd written, reading it but not really reading it because I couldn't concentrate.

I wondered if I should call him Edward if I ever spoke to him. Or if it was only teachers who called him that, and maybe his parents too.

I wondered what would happen if I had to shout after him if he ever dropped his bus pass. I imagined myself shouting, "Eddie!" in the corridor, waving his bus pass in the air, while everyone laughed at me, shouting, "Who's *Eddie*? Do you mean Ed?!"

And then I felt something tap me lightly on my arm. It was Eddie! He was staring straight ahead at Mrs Kelp, but his arm was stretched out towards me. He was trying to pass me a note!

I looked at Mrs Kelp and slowly put my hand out to take the note. But I couldn't find his hand right away, and ended up touching his arm a couple of times and going BRIGHT RED before I eventually got the note.

I gripped the note in my hand under the desk, scared to do anything other than that in case my face burst like an out-of-date tomato.

Eventually I calmed down a bit, and was just about to look at the note when Mrs Kelp said, "OK. That's time up. Everyone out. Except for you, Peri. You've got a double."

Although I was a bit gutted that Edward was gone, I also felt massively relieved. I was now on my own, and that meant I could read the note Edward had written me without him looking at me while I read it.

I waited until Mrs Kelp began furiously typing again before slowly unfolding Edward's note.

Although I was basically alone, I felt my face and neck burn with embarrassment as I read:

DEATH BY CHOCOLATE ORANGE

LESSON — TRY TO HAVE A NORMAL GRAN (IT'S MUCH EASIER)

That weekend I decided I couldn't face seeing Cammy. I mean, she wasn't AT ALL embarrassed by what had happened in the cafeteria (which terrified me) and I couldn't stop feeling angry at her every time I thought about the horrible note Edward had written me. I had TOLD Cammy the dance was a bad idea, but she just HAD to go ahead and do it anyway, didn't she? And it's just like Cammy to do whatever she wants and not care about how I feel.

So as soon as I woke up on Saturday morning, I went to visit my gran so Cammy wouldn't be able to find me and physically *pull* me into another one of her "brilliant ideas".

NIGHTMARES I Had About Other Ways Cammy Might Try to Get Us "Noticed"

1 Cammy drags me into a police station, saying we have committed a murder.

2 Cammy replaces the buttons and zips on my clothes with poppers. She then waits until we're walking through a mobbed corridor at school and rips all my clothes off in one giant pull.

3 I can't really remember the third nightmare, but I know it had something to do with Cammy stealing my teeth and making some sort of "touch-and-feel" pop-up book. (Note to self: NEVER eat triple-cheese nachos before bed AGAIN!)

So anyway, I decided to hide at my gran's.

This may not have been the best plan.

I left feeling more stressed out than when I arrived.

I guess that's just what my family does to me.

(I should point out here that my gran isn't really a normal, sweet, "granny-ish" gran who says things like, "Oh! You're getting so tall these days!" or "Would you like a biscuit?".)

My visit went a bit like this:

"How are your legs today, Gran?"

Gran has bad legs. I don't actually know what's wrong with them, they're just bad. Gran's got a bad back too, and a bad heart, the doctor says.

"Oh, they're bad. Bad, bad, bad," said Gran.

Poor Gran.

"Can I get you anything, Gran? A cup of tea? A biscuit? A Terry's Chocolate Orange?"

Chocolate Oranges are Gran's favourite. I proudly produce one from my bag. I am in fact campaigning for Granddaughter of the Year.

It might sound like a terrible thing to say, but I want to be Gran's favourite and I'm currently competing against my (very annoying) big cousin Luke who's training to be a doctor and my three-year-old little cousin who has blonde pigtails and says things like, "I wuv woo, Wanny". So the gloves are off.

"Awww, you're a wee pet, aren't you? Looking after an old, frail bag-of-bones like me."

I love my gran.

"Here you go, Gran. I'll open it for you. How many segments would you—"

"SSSSSHHHHH!" she hisses.

"What? What is it, Gran?"

Gran drops suddenly to the floor.

Oh my God! It must be her heart!

"SSSSHHH! Stop yapping and GET DOWN!"

Oh, thank God. She's alive.

"What are you *DOING*, Gran?"

I am pulled to the ground.

"That nosy witch across the road is at it again!"

I lie on the carpet and watch as Gran crawls commando-style across the living-room floor towards the lamp.

We are now in darkness.

"Gran, are you OK?"

Gran races across the room and looks through her net curtains.

Her "bad" legs seem much better.

"LOOK! Come and see this nosy parker across the street. She's watching us!"

Aren't we watching her too?

"She is OBSESSED with me. OBSESSED, I tell you," Gran hisses.

Did I mention my gran's a bit mad?

And now she's got binoculars. Perfect.

"Stupid woman! She's forgotten to turn her kitchen light off. I can see right in!"

I'm pretty sure people can get arrested for this.

"OH THE DEVIL! She's copied my curtains! Those are my EXACT curtains. LOOK!"

Why is this happening to me? Why can't I just have a nice normal gran who gives you cuddles and watches the TV?

"Gran, can we put the light back on now?"

"Well, we'll have to shut these curtains first or

she'll know what colour underwear we're wearing in no time. The nosy thing."

I help Gran "secure" the curtains.

She looks livid.

"I bet that nosy woman thinks I'll have to go out and get new kitchen curtains now, doesn't she? Well, I won't give her the satisfaction!"

Is it terrible that I want to shove the whole Chocolate Orange in her mouth? Just to shut her up?

"OK, Gran, that's nice. I better get going. Um, I think Cammy's looking for me."

TUNA BALL

LESSON — NEVER, EVER, EVER TALK WITH YOUR MOUTH FULL

Cammy sent me a text on Monday morning before school:

HI PERI. WHERE WERE YOU ALL WEEKEND?! NEED TO SEE YOU ASAP. P.S. I WON'T BE IN SCHOOL TODAY. GETTING NEW BRACES FITTED.

I was mammothly relieved when I found out that Cammy wouldn't be at school. I mean, things were going to be bad enough for me when I saw Edward after the "note" incident on Friday, without me having to worry that Cammy was going to inflict even more crazy upon the school.

154

But then, at lunch, something crazy *DID* happen.
Something I did NOT expect.

Out of nowhere …

EDWARD
SAT
NEXT TO ME!

"Hi, Peri."

Oh my God … he remembers my NAME! Wait I hate him now.

"So, where's Cammy? You two not performing together today?"

And then he grinned at me.

Is he making fun of me again? To my FACE?

I was JUST about to explode when he said, "So, what did your secret note say? I hope it was worth me risking another detention for!"

Oh my God. He didn't write it! It must have been one of the poopulars. Of COURSE!

"Oh. Err. It was just about the dancing thing yesterday."

I CANNOT believe I just told him that. I CANNOT tell him what it said.

"So, why exactly *did* you guys start dancing in the cafeteria?"

"It wasn't just a dance, you know. It was for charity."

Oh my God. What am I saying?

"Oh. Right. I didn't know that."

Why would you? IT'S A LIE!

"So how much did you raise?"

"Five hundred pounds."

SHUT UP SHUT UP SHUT UP SHUT UP!

"WOW! *Really?*" he said.

NO!

"Yes," I lied.

"That's unbelievable!"

"Yet, very believable."

I have a disease.

"Which charity?"

"Sorry?"

Oh my God. I cannot think of a charity. Not ONE!

"Which charity are you giving the money to?"

Oh no, no, no, no! Think, think, think, think, think!

"The Dinner Ladies' Foundation."

AAAAAAARRRRRRRGGGGGGG!

"The what?!"

And now he's looking at me with a really weird look on his face.

"The Dinner Ladies' Foundation. So they can get new ladles. For the soup."

WHAT am I saying?!

"Oh. Erm. OK."

I can't breathe. Change the subject.

"So I see you didn't get the soup. Was that because you didn't like the look of the ladles?"

STOP TALKING ABOUT LADLES! WHAT'S WRONG WITH YOU??!

"Erm, no. I just wanted a sandwich."

Now he thinks I'm obsessed with ladles. Great job, Peri!

"Mmmmm … ham … yummy. Is that your favourite?"

I shouldn't be allowed to talk to people.

"Erm, I suppose so. What do you have?"

I can't believe he's still sitting here talking to me. Maybe he's too scared to get up in case I run after him and beat him to death with a ladle. STOP THINKING ABOUT LADLES! Think about sandwiches. OK. What did he ask me again? What's in my sandwich. OK. Oh my God. I'm looking right at it, and I have NO IDEA what it is.

"Oh. I don't know what's in it. I'll have to taste it."

I think I'm having an out-of-body experience.

Thank God I've remembered how to eat. Take a bite. Good. Now chew. What does it taste like? Uh-oh. That was too much. Oh my God. Some just fell out of my mouth. It's tuna. It's definitely tuna. I can see it on my skirt.

Oh my God. STOP DRIBBLING TUNA ALL OVER YOURSELF!

STOP EVERYTHING!!!

And now I'm choking. Properly choking. Hand slapping on the table, face going red, lips turning blue, choking.

And then it all started to get a bit fuzzy. But I do remember my PE teacher, Miss Gretcher, lifting me off my seat and squeezing my ribs until a huge tuna ball shot out of my mouth and on to the table.

Right in front of Edward.

And then I died inside.

Later that day...

That night I decided to go and see Cammy. I mean, I didn't really care about her next crazy plan to get us noticed any more. It didn't matter now. Nothing could be worse than what I'd already done to myself that day.

Cammy seemed really excited to see me. She ran down to get us both yoghurts and told me that she wanted to hear all about what I'd been up to since Friday.

So I told her about Gran and the woman across the road with the curtains, and she laughed LOADS and said she wished she'd been there, which made me feel a bit guilty.

Then I told her about what had happened at lunch with the tuna ball. And about how we somehow now had to raise £500 and give it to the dinner ladies.

"Why ladles?" said Cammy. "Do you like them?"

"I don't know why, Cammy! That's what I'm telling you. I went mad, I tell you. MAD!"

"It's just, if you'd said spoons that would've helped promote our band."

"I wasn't really thinking about that at the time, Cammy. I was a bit, well, nervous, you know?"

"Why were you nervous?" asked Cammy. She was clearly oblivious to the fact that I liked Edward, or that he was awesome.

"It doesn't matter," I said. I could feel my face start to burn again.

"So, go on, show me the rest of your 'unique' ideas for the band," I said.

Cammy's eyes lit up and she pulled her notepad out and started drawing things that made me laugh.

"What IS that?" I asked.

"Spoon-trousers," said Cammy matter-of-factly. And then we both burst out laughing.

SOMETIMES THINGS JUST GET OUT OF CONTROL

LESSON — DO NOT MESS WITH WORDS (YOU MAY CAUSE A SERIOUS ACCIDENT)

So, today was weird. And it went from weird to weirder.

WEIRD

I was walking to History when Edward stopped me and asked if I was OK.

I immediately began checking my shirt for chocolate milk, under my shoes for toilet roll and my nose for bleeding.

"I'm talking about the choking thing, yesterday," Edward said. "You know? Your 'near-death by tuna'?"

I burst out laughing. He laughed too. I was

surprised that I was actually able to laugh about the tuna-ball incident.

"I'm fine, thanks. Sorry about that," I said, suddenly feeling awkward again as I visualised the tuna-ball landing on the table in front of him.

"So, how's the band going?" Edward asked.

The awkward feeling began to spread up towards my neck. I had no idea what to say. No, that's not true. I definitely wanted to let him know how much I'd wanted him to be in our band, and how annoyed I was with Cammy for sending him away. But I had no idea how to translate that into actual sentences that didn't make it sound like I was obsessed with him.

So I settled for, "It's OK, thanks."

He continued to smile at me, but I noticed that he looked the tiniest bit disappointed.

And then all of a sudden Cammy was there. I hadn't actually noticed her arrive.

"Can I ask you a quick question about your foot eczema, Peri?" she asked.

Edward glanced down at my feet.

I literally couldn't think of anything to say. And then Edward said he had to go, and Cammy dragged me into the loo and started showing me her feet.

That afternoon in History things started to get out of hand. Mr Galloway kept saying the word "POVERTY" over and over again, and it sounded weird because of his Irish accent.

He said it so much that I couldn't really concentrate on any of the other words he was saying. I just kept waiting for him to say "POVERTY" again. Then I started to think about the word "POVERTY" *way* too much. And that made me need to say it quietly to myself quite a lot.

But then I said it so much that it started to sound *really* weird, and I couldn't remember how to say it the way that didn't sound weird, because the way I was saying it sounded new (and also a bit like a pirate). And then I noticed Cammy staring at me.

"Are you *OK*?"

"Not really," I said. "How do you say 'poverty'? I've forgotten."

"What?"

"*Poverty.* The *word*. How do you say it?"

"What do you mean? You just said it!"

"So you understood me then? I'm saying it right?"

"Err, yes. Are you feeling OK?"

But then I couldn't say any more because Mr Galloway flicked his hair at us, which is quite impressive since he doesn't really have any. Well, he does, but it's only a little slimy bit on the top of his head, and it doesn't exactly slope over his face into his eyes or anything. So it's certainly nothing that he would need to "flick". But that doesn't seem to stop him.

Anyway, once Mr Galloway was done flicking or twitching or whatever he was doing, I tried to explain to Cammy all about the "POVERTY" thing. But Cammy wasn't really getting it, and that's when things started to get out of hand.

It went a bit like this:

"Say '*POVERTY*', Cammy."

"Poverty."

"Now say it again, over and over."

"Why?"

"Just do it!"

"Poverty, poverty, poverty, poverty."

But she wasn't getting it. I could tell by her face.

"Can I stop now?"

"Fine."

Trust Cammy NOT to get something TOTALLY obvious.

"Do you not think some words sound weird, Cammy? I mean, who decided that 'poverty' should be a word anyway? I mean, what *IS* poverty?"

And that's when Mr Galloway came rushing over.

"What a BRILLIANT question, Pero!"

Long story. Well, not really. Mr Galloway just thinks my name is Pero. I told him on the first day that it wasn't. And he apologised. But then he must've forgotten. And now I can't be bothered to bring it up again.

"Sorry, sir ... what question?"

I had no idea what he was talking about.

"What *IS* poverty, Pero? What a brilliant question! Let's have a class discussion right now!"

I thought about trying to explain to Mr Galloway that I knew exactly what poverty meant, and that it was just the actual *word* I was having trouble with, but if Cammy didn't get what I was talking about, then I doubted Mr Galloway would.

The debate started off OK. People kind of adopted this way of talking about poverty that made it a lot easier to think of something to say when it was your turn.

For example people said things like:

Poverty is not having enough food.

Poverty is living off one pence a day.

Poverty is being homeless.

So everything was going fine. And I had my "Poverty is…" sentence for discussion all ready. But then this really snooty kid who sits beside me put up his hand and said:

"Poverty is being so poor you cannot afford proper school shoes." And then he looked at Bobby Hammer's feet and smirked.

And Bobby Hammer went BERSERK. Proper berserk. First he started shouting at the snooty kid and telling him to shut his "stupid posh face" and then he started laughing at him and calling him "Sir Snooty-Pants the third". Then he kicked a chair over. And then he started crying.

Then, Angela McAllister started screaming,

"THAT CHAIR ALMOST TOUCHED ME! I COULD HAVE BEEN KNOCKED UNCONSCIOUS!" And she ran from the class and went right to the head teacher and said she had been caught in the middle of a "hate crime" between the rich and the poor. She's a nightmare.

So then we all had to be interviewed individually by the head, and tell him EXACTLY what had happened in class.

So I explained all about how this whole mess started, and about how *strange* the word "poverty" is, and then I asked the head if he would say it over and over again, so I could show him what I was talking about, but he wouldn't. And then he asked me to leave.

In the end, both Bobby and "Sir Snooty-Pants the third" got detention (even though the whole thing was pretty much my fault, if you think about it).

PETUNIA PERRY: THUG & HOOLIGAN

LESSON — NEVER UNDERESTIMATE A MOTHER'S ABILITY TO CRUSH THE HUMAN SOUL

When I got home that day, Mum sat me down and said that the head teacher had called (brilliant) and that he'd said I'd been acting strangely in his office today. He also mentioned the "spoon thing". AND the double-detention thing.

I decided not to even bother trying to explain, because my mother always just makes up her own mind about what she "thinks" has happened anyway. And there's NO arguing with her, so what's the point?

So when she asked me why I'd been acting so strangely in the head's office, I just said, "I was acting strange because I'm strange." But Mum wouldn't let it go.

It wasn't a fun conversation:

"Peri. My sweet angel. Have you joined a terrible gang?"

"No, Mum."

"You can tell me. I'm your mother. Dad and I will always love you. No matter what."

I can't believe this is happening.

"No, Mum. Of COURSE I've not joined a 'terrible gang'. I'm eleven."

"Well, is it woman troubles then?"

I should have just said I was in a gang.

"No, Mum. And would you please, please stop asking me about that every five seconds."

"Well, what is it then? Are you being bullied? OH MY GOODNESS! THAT'S IT, ISN'T IT? YOU'RE BEING BULLIED! MY ANGEL IS BEING BULLIED BY THUGS AND HOOLIGANS!"

I suppose I should just be thankful that I have a mother who seems to care about me so much.

But I am not.

"Mum, listen. I am NOT being bullied. Well, not really. I mean, people laugh at me sometimes, but—"

"Give me their names."

"What?"

"Their NAMES, Peri. Give them to me."

All of a sudden she has a pen and paper.

"I don't know their names. Look, it's nothing serious. I mean, it's just high-school stuff. It doesn't bother me."

"Well, when you *do* get bullied, Peri—"

"Wait. Don't you mean *if*? *IF* I get bullied?"

"Well, you *are* a bit different."

Here we go.

"And sometimes people don't appreciate 'different'. Not like I do."

EH?

When has my mother ever appreciated me being different? I distinctly remember her throwing a tantrum when I transformed my ballet tutu into a very useful parachute for my dinosaurs.

Also, is it possible that she is SO mad that she doesn't even realise a large portion of the laughing and pointing at school is

due to HER shenanigans on Parents' Evening?

THANKFULLY I managed to change the subject from "terrible gangs" and non-existent bullies to my upcoming twelfth birthday.

Mum got really excited when I brought it up. Mum LOVES birthdays.

She began asking me the same questions she asks me EVERY year (even though she knows the answers). For example:

Mum: What cake would you like this year?
Me: Colin the Caterpillar, please!
Mum: The one from Marks & Spencer?
Me: Of course.
Mum: Wonderful!
Me: Thanks, Mum.

But then she got a weird look in her eye.
I should have KNOWN she was up to something.

IT'S MY PARTY
AND I'LL DIE IF
I WANT TO

A few days later I found out why Mum had been so excited about my twelfth birthday. She was planning a surprise party for me (she's quite sweet sometimes, I suppose).

Cammy accidentally spilled the beans at school the day before the party when I suggested we go to her house to practise on my birthday.

At first I panicked a little, because Cammy looked at me weird when I suggested it, and then she looked at Cara. I thought maybe they'd planned to do something without me, and that they'd just been found out or something.

But then Cammy blurted out, "I can't do this! I

don't DO lies! Your mum's throwing you a surprise party."

And that's how I found out.

That night I kept freaking Mum and Dad out by sneaking up on them to see what they were up to. It was hilarious listening to all the rubbish lies they came up with.

For example, I caught Mum blowing up balloons in the utility room (the door has frosted glass – she clearly didn't think it through) and she tried to tell me I had to run to the garage and help Dad RIGHT AWAY as he was having an (unexplained) emergency. I walked out of the kitchen to find Dad sleeping on the sofa.

I was actually quite looking forward to my birthday party. I'd assumed that it would probably just be the family and Cammy, and Cammy's mum. And Cara, I guessed. And that we'd have a big dinner together, eat cake, laugh and listen to music.

But I was wrong.

I mean, I know it's really nice that Mum wants to make me feel special on my birthday. But she DOES know that I don't really like a fuss. So why does she ALWAYS have to take things too far?

So what happened is that I walked home with Cammy and Cara after school to find that all the blinds were shut and the lights were off.

We went inside and as I walked into the dark living room (pretending I couldn't see the human-shaped lumps at the side of the couch) I prepared to act surprised.

But it turned out I didn't need to pretend because Mum gave me the fright of my life when she appeared ninja-style at my side and screamed, "SURPRISE!" into my face. I almost had a heart attack.

And then the lights went on and everyone started singing happy birthday to me. It was nice (even though they were making quite a big fuss).

But then as I looked around the room my positivity was challenged.

I realised that there were quite a few faces I'd genuinely never seen before. I started to panic because I absolutely HATE being in the position when someone knows you, and your name, but you don't know THEIR name, so you try to hide it and be super-happy to see them but then you can TELL by their face that they've clocked what's going on, and they know that you don't know their name (or who they are) and that you're just pretending. And then YOU know that THEY know that YOU know. It's horrible.

After the party, I found out that Cammy had been in charge of inviting people from school. And that she'd decided to hand out "plus-one" invites, because obviously she is crazy and thought that she was inviting people to a wedding or something, instead of a twelfth birthday party. I wish she'd told me this at the time, but she didn't. So I walked round the room, thanking everyone for coming and saying stupid stuff like, "It's nice to see you again" (when clearly I had probably never seen them before in my life).

A few people turned up late and every time the doorbell rang I wondered which random Fortress person was going to walk into my living room next. Jessica Clark? Mr Phart? The lollipop man?!

So I was VERY pleasantly surprised when one of the latecomers was Edward!

However, I almost choked on my own tongue when Max Martin walked into my living room.

"MAX!" Mum screamed. "I'm so pleased you could make it!"

I'd been hoping she'd forgotten about the whole Max Martin-boyfriend nonsense. But obviously she hadn't.

"Hello, Peri," said Max in his annoyingly Max Martin-ish voice. "So sorry I couldn't be here earlier. I had a hospital appointment about my rash."

And then he handed me a rose.

I was unable to talk due to the fact that I had swallowed my own tongue.

I pulled my jumper sleeve over my hand a bit and carefully took the rose without touching his skin.

"*Peri!* Max gave you a *gift*," Mum whisper-hissed. "What do you *saaay*?"

What DO I say? I thought. I honestly had no idea.

How about:

"Thank you very much for NOT drawing my face

on this rose?"

"Why are you in my house?"

"WHAT THE FRYING PAN IS GOING ON???!!!"

"So … are you surprised, honey?" said Mum. "I invited Max specially."

And then she started giggling.

Then Max started giggling too.

Great. Now my mum and Max Martin are BFFs.

"I have something else for you," said Max, and then he ran out into the hall.

I probably should have known what was about to happen.

But I didn't.

I guess I'm a glass half-full sort of person and this world is just too cruel for me.

"Could someone give me a hand with this, please? It's heavy," he said. And then he grinned at me through his goggles (FYI – Max Martin wears the kind of glasses that have "straps" rather than "legs". Even though he plays no sports whatsoever).

The MINUTE Max said "this", Cammy gripped my hand and I knew why. She was thinking the same thing I was thinking. And we were right.

"SURPRISE!" Max and Mum screamed in unison.

Max and Mum. Mum and Max. Oh God. It's starting to sound like a "thing" now. Like they're a team, or a couple of cute bears in a kid's picture book.

One day, Max and Mum went for a picnic. But Max forgot his sunhat, so Mum had to make him a hat out of leaves. Max looked just like a tree. Oh, how they laughed.

Urrgh.

Anyway…

"NO!" Cammy said (a bit too loudly) when Mum helped Max into the living room with a LAAAAAARGE, wrapped square-ish gift.

I KNEW that Mum wouldn't let me get away with not opening it in front of everyone. Plus she was visibly salivating since she obviously knew it was another "unicorn-fiasco".

"On you go, Peri. Open it," said Mum. "Everyone wants to see what your boyfriend has got you for your birthday."

I'd actually lost count of how many times I'd told Mum that Max WASN'T my boyfriend. She was unbelievable.

I side-glanced at Edward as I walked towards the

"gift". He didn't look very happy (which made me a bit happier).

"Mum, *please.* Max isn't my boyfriend."

"OK, fine, fine," said Mum, winking at Max. Max grinned maniacally at me.

I decided to approach this situation like a "plaster-on-your-knee" incident. Quick and painful. But then it's (almost) over.

I grabbed the wrapping paper with both hands and ripped it all off in one go.

Even though I thought I was prepared (I mean, I'd already seen one of these paintings before) I was NOT prepared for THIS.

I didn't think it was possible, but this painting was WAY WORSE than the original.

It was like looking directly into the mind of a future serial killer.

Unicorn-me appeared to have human hands.

And a large pink diamond on its WEDDING RING FINGER!

Unicorn-Max was holding a single red rose in his weirdly morphed hand-hoof.

And to my absolute horror, we both appeared to have loads of little love hearts shooting out of our eyes, ears … and BOTTOMS!

I started to feel dizzy.

And the dizziness got worse when I noticed that there were loads of BABY UNICORNS frolicking around us.

And for some deeply disturbing reason, they all looked EXACTLY like Cammy!

Cammy looked horrified.

"Um, um, I have to nip out for a minute," she said. And then she rushed out of the front door and ran past the living-room window. I knew she was going to check that Margaret was OK.

Even Mum's smile flickered a bit when she saw it.

I couldn't handle this.

"There's NO WAY that's going up in my room!" I shouted before I'd realised what I was saying.

I felt (slightly) guilty when Max's eyes started to fill with water.

"I ... I ... I thought we had a special connection, Peri," Max whimpered.

Special connection?! I have spoken to this person TWICE in my life.

"PERI! Look what you've done!" Mum yelled as she ushered Max through to the kitchen.

Everyone stood and stared at me and the painting in silence until Mum and Max reappeared.

Max had a tissue stuffed up his nose.

Mum had her arm around him.

"Max has had a nosebleed," Mum announced solemnly. "And he's fatally allergic to pork, cheese and white bread."

I had no idea how these things were connected. I mean, had she tried to stop the bleeding by shoving a cheese sandwich up there or something?!

"So," said Mum as she took Max by the hand, "if everyone could please step away from the cheese sandwiches and cocktail sausages, I'll have to put them in the outside bin immediately. Then we can all have some lovely crackers and fruit. Won't that be fun?"

Yes. Yes it will.

If fun means an experience similar to having your hair set on fire.

Just then Max sneezed, and blood splattered all over Mum's cream sofa.

Mum's smile went really tight. She let go of Max's hand.

"OK!" said Dad, clearly sensing that Mum's feelings towards Max had shifted. "Maria, why don't we get this party started!"

And that's when Mum tried to pretend that she wasn't screaming on the inside about the blood on her couch and announced that the "fun" was about to start.

Then Dad put on some really loud music and Cara walked up and handed me three cocktail sausages (directly from her hand, no napkin required, apparently).

"Here. Take these before your mum purges the house of tastiness! Happy birthday."

I smiled at her gratefully but before I could say anything, Edward appeared.

"Hi," he said. "Happy birthday, Peri."

"Thank you," I whispered.

He handed me a small box.

I held it in my non-smuggled-sausage hand.

"Sorry about all the tape. Um, you might want to just leave it and open it later," he said, looking a bit nervous.

He was right about the tape. He must've used a whole roll.

"Thanks," I managed to say.

Before I could even consider opening it, Cara took the gift out of my hand and said she would put it with the other presents. And then it was just me and Edward. Standing in the middle of my living room.

I was suddenly very aware of the (x 3) cocktail sausages I was still gripping in my hand. And before I knew what I was doing I'd put them in my mouth. All of them.

So of course, that's when Edward started talking to me again.

"You know, I don't actually play the spoons," he said, smiling at me. "I just wanted to join your band.

I thought maybe I could talk you into letting me play my guitar instead, but then Cara turned up and she was awesome."

I just stood there staring at him, chewing all of the cocktail sausages as slowly as I could, willing myself not to choke (again).

Just then the front door slammed shut and Cammy came rushing over.

"Margaret's fine this time. She's totally fine," she gasped.

"Thank goodness!" I said without thinking. (Without remembering about the sausages.)

"Excuse me," I spluttered as I rushed off to get a napkin. Great. I'd spat sausage on myself. On my birthday. In front of Edward. I was officially the most disgusting human ever.

When I got back, Cammy was speaking to Edward. Max was there now too. He was still bleeding.

"The Spoons could DEFINITELY use a guitar player!" said Cammy, waving Cara over. I was thrilled. This was the best birthday present EVER!

"Awesome!" said Edward. "I'm an official Spoon now, I guess."

Then Max stepped forward and opened his mouth

to say something and I just KNEW that he was going to try to join the band, and that Cammy might just be mad enough to let him. But then Mum saved me. Well, sort of. She began clapping her hands and asking for everyone's attention.

"OK, everyone! Gather round!"

"It's time for … LANZO THE FANTASTICO!" my mum screamed.

I audibly gulped at this point.

The next three minutes were the worst of my life.

I didn't know who this Lanzo person was, but in the three minutes it took for Mum to wrestle open the kitchen door (and moan about having asked Dad to fix it a million times) I completely and utterly tortured myself.

Some of the torturous thoughts that went through my mind in those three minutes

1 Lanzo is a clown.
2 Lanzo is a kids' magician.
3 Lanzo is some sort of creepy ventriloquist's dummy.

4 Lanzo is a lion who is going to eat us all alive (this was my favourite option).

And then the door opened.

The next three minutes made the previous three minutes look like a wonderland of fun:

"WELL, HELLOOOOO, BOYS AND GIRLS! I'm Lanzo the Fantasticoooo! And this is my beautiful assistant, Star!"

Cammy gasped and actually dropped her Coke on the ground.

OH.

MY.

GOD.

My little cousin started crying.

I looked around at everyone from school. I was somehow hoping they weren't seeing this.

They were.

"Don't cry, Toby," said Mum. "It's just Uncle Perry

dressed up as a magical clown! Nothing to cry about!"

Nothing to cry about? NOTHING TO CRY ABOUT??!

My father was wearing what can only be described as a woman's dress, and Cammy's mum had a glittery bikini on!

I'd like to point out here that as much as I DO love my mum and am grateful for her efforts, I think it's fair to say that you should NEVER have to have any of the following at your twelfth surprise birthday party:

1 A magical clown who's also your dad

2 A banner that says, "You're Almost a Teenager, My Baby Angel"

3 THE BOY YOU LIKE (due to 1 & 2)

4 Max Martin

"Now, for my first trick I shall make one of you disappear!" said Lanzo.

I cannot tell you how much I wished my dad could have made ME disappear in that moment.

"Can I have a volunteer from the audience, please?"

Nobody volunteered.

Everyone was still in shock.

Dad repeated his question.

Funnily enough, *nobody* volunteered.

I looked around to see some people from school were talking pictures of "Lanzo" on their phones. Great. Now my "Super-cool4kidz" birthday party would be all over the Internet and EVERYBODY at school would know just how much of a freak my dad is.

"I'll do it!" shouted Mum.

Of course she will.

So we all just stood there as Dad put Mum into an old cardboard box and watched as "Star" put a sheet over the box and said a "magic chant".

Then we all watched as a rather large lump "escaped" from the box and crawled really quickly into the kitchen.

"TA DA!"

Then Cammy's mum sang a song about the Earth. And we were all given a (much deserved!) slice of Colin the Caterpillar. And then, at last, it was over.

Later that night Mum called me downstairs and asked me to sit with her on the (newly cleaned) couch. And then she said that maybe I should think about BREAKING UP with Max Martin since she felt he was a bit "high-maintenance".

I am beginning to think that my mother might drink shampoo. It would explain so much.

THE EYE
OF JESSICA
CLARK

I turned up at school on Monday expecting to find pictures of my dad dressed up as "creepy-woman's-dress-wearing-Lanzo" all over the school. But thankfully there were none.

Instead of feeling relieved, this made me very nervous.

I mean, I'd definitely seen people take pictures so I guessed it was just a matter of time before they appeared.

But then Cara came over and cheered me up instantly. She said that Edward had asked her in registration when our next practice was, and that she'd told him it was today at lunch and that we'd meet him in the cafeteria.

We met Edward at the baked-potato station. He was in the middle of being served when we arrived.

"What do you think, Peri? Is the tuna too risky?" he said, then laughed and put his arm round my shoulders in the same jokey way he'd done before.

I laughed too. The dinner lady did NOT.

"Do you want a 'tato or not?" she snapped.

Edward apologised and asked if he could please have a cheese baked potato to go.

He was so charming that by the time she handed him his "tato" she was smiling. I was shocked. I'd never seen one of them do that before, ever.

That's when I realised that I probably wasn't the only one who liked Edward so much. He was confident, well mannered and you could tell he was also a really good guy.

"What 'bout you?" the dinner lady said to me in her "back-to-normal" way.

"Um. No thanks, I've got a packed lunch," I said. The moment I said it, I wished I hadn't. She'd clearly taken it as a personal insult.

As we headed out of the cafeteria towards the

Music department, I was very aware that people were looking at us. And I knew that it was only partly because Cammy had started eating the largest piece of lettuce I had ever seen, directly from her bag. It was mostly because Edward was with us. *US!* (The Spoons.)

The school cafeteria suddenly felt like the largest place in the world. As we eventually reached the exit, we had to walk past the poopular table. I tried not to look because I was feeling mega-nervous, but of course I did, and caught Jessica's eye. She looked furious.

Now, I know you're probably thinking, "GOOD! Well done, Peri! She's a horrible person who crowned you Ugly Pigeon and she deserves to watch you be with Edward when she likes him too. ENJOY IT!"

But I didn't feel like that at ALL. I felt a bit like she was planning something completely embarrassing that would make Edward laugh at me and not want to join our band.

To make an awkward moment worse, Edward and Cammy burst out laughing at something Cara said while we were walking out of the door, and Edward didn't hear Jessica say, "Hi, Edward, how are you?" And all I could think was:

Someone is going to have to pay for that. And I bet it's me.

A COMPLETE SET OF SPOONS!

Our first practice together went well, though I didn't really feel like I was performing to the best of my ability, and I knew it was because I was holding back a little so Edward didn't think I was weird.

Cammy and Cara on the other hand were going MAD. They sounded awesome and had managed to synchronise their percussion to almost perfection.

When Edward had said he played guitar, I had instantly expected it to be a big, flashy electric guitar, but it wasn't. It was a battered old acoustic guitar, and he was SO good at playing it that I, somehow, felt even MORE self-conscious.

Edward seemed really interested in my keyboard, and Cammy was BEGGING me to show him the crazy song we'd come up with the other day, but I wasn't sure he would like it, so I made an excuse and said that we should wait and show him with Margaret there too.

Edward looked a bit confused. "Who's Margaret?" he asked. "Is she in our year?"

And that's when I realised we hadn't actually told Edward about the fourth member of our band.

Suddenly the best, most amazingly perfect and fabulous idea in the world seemed a teeny, tiny bit embarrassing. I watched Edward's face closely as Cammy explained ALL about Margaret and her "abilities", and how she would be performing live with us. And then explained that we were pretty sure she was the reincarnation of Elvis.

Edward looked at us all for a second, and for a moment I felt like I was seeing the three of us through someone else's eyes. We were definitely crazy, weren't we? Weirdos. Freaks. Perhaps even losers?

But then Edward grinned at me and said, "I need to meet this cat IMMEDIATELY."

And I've literally NEVER been so relieved in ALL of my life. Edward was one of us!

That evening Cammy invited us all to her house for a full band practice. I was beyond excited. I felt amazing.

Cammy's mum had broken one of her sacred fast-food rules and ordered us all pizza (I have NO idea how Cammy managed to talk her into that one) and even though it was some sort of Mediterranean pizza from the fancy restaurant down the road, I was delighted (and absolutely STARVING since I'd skipped lunch).

Me, Cammy and Cara were already in Cammy's room by the time Edward arrived. He looked even more gorgeous out of school than he did in it.

Just then, Margaret came sauntering into the room.

"Wow. This must be the lady herself!" said Edward, crouching down to look at her.

"Pleased to meet you, miss," he said, and held out his hand. Margaret sniffed it for AGES and then began licking it. Margaret is a VERY good judge of character!

Edward looked at me and smiled. "Can I show you something?"

And then he went to his bag and pulled out what I thought was the tiniest guitar I'd ever seen, until I realised it was a ukulele.

"I thought Margaret might like the sound of it," he said, and began playing a little tune. Margaret did. She started to ad-lib like MAD.

Edward laughed until he had tears streaming down his face.

"She's AMAZING!" he beamed as he stroked her. And then she began licking his hand again.

The rest of the practice was perfect. We all went WILD. Cammy and I managed to get back into our crazy jam-sesh mood and showed Cara and Edward

our "unique" creation. Both Cara and Edward seemed to have no problem coming up with something that fitted in, and Margaret yowled, chattered and wailed in perfect harmony with us. That's when I realised we'd actually done it. We had made a band. A good band. An awesome band!

We were The Spoons!

PAWTOGRAPHS

The next day at school I heard someone running up behind me and Cammy on the way to registration. I completely panicked and pulled Cammy to one side, assuming it was Jessica, or one of her popular army, about to attack us with hairspray or something.

I was relieved (and mega-excited!) to see that it was Edward. He looked so cute. My face went red instantly.

"You've had your hair cut," said Cammy.

And he had. It sat neatly over to the side now instead of flopping into his eyes.

"I had to," he said, beaming with excitement. "I want to be able to see the crowd clearly when they're shouting our name tomorrow night."

I was confused. So was Cammy.

"What crowd?" we both said at the same time.

"OUR crowd," he said. "I got us a GIG!"

Shock number one: Edward's gorgeous new hair.

Shock number two: What he'd actually said!

Cammy was practically bouncing off the walls with excitement. Mr Burton actually had to tell her to keep her voice down and to sit still while he took the register.

The reality of the fact that Edward had actually managed to get us a real, live gig, and the even MORE real fact that it was in less than forty-eight hours was beginning to freak me out.

"Cammy, I don't think we're ready," I said.

"Of course we are!" she squealed, and instantly got told off by Mr Burton.

"Peri," Cammy said in a more normal tone when Mr Burton had gone back to droning on about something else. "The Spoons are ready. We sounded like the best band I have ever heard in my life last night."

And she was right. It had been awesome.

Cammy then said that she believed it was a very good thing that our first gig was so soon, and explained to me about the dangers of over-rehearsing.

We were over the moon that Edward had managed not only to secure us our first ever live gig, but that he'd managed to get us into a completely "unique" venue. I mean, how many bands do their first gig in a bowling alley? Probably none. Until now!

Edward had said that he'd managed to book a venue with a stage at the back that was usually used for fundraisers. It sounded awesome!

Earlier, we'd managed to meet as a band (minus Margaret) in the music cupboard at lunch, and agreed on a short set list of three songs (since Edward said we only had a twenty-minute slot before the bingo started).

SET LIST

Track 1: Everyone does a 1-min solo each and then we all do our solos at the same time for 1 min (5 mins)
Track 2: Edward and Cara do an awesome fast track together, just the two of them (4 mins)

Track 3: Cammy brings Margaret on to the stage and introduces her as the fifth band member. We then do our bonkers tune as a whole band, with Margaret ad-libbing like MAD (6 mins)

Once Cammy's mum had agreed that we could take Margaret to the gig (as long as she drove us there and back and Margaret was kept on her long kitty-lead) we were massively relieved.

Everything was coming together. Our hard work was paying off. The world was our oyster!

As for band merchandise, we had eight T-shirts with Margaret's face on them, five mugs and a LOT of socks.

So we made the following executive band decisions:

Executive Band Decisions

1 We would each wear one of the T-shirts and sell the remaining four after the gig to our fans.

2 We didn't have time (or resources) to get flyers made up to promote our gig so we'd have to settle for a few posters, which we could put up around the school.

3 We would **NOT** be organising a sock raffle at the end of our gig. (I was forced to use my one and only "NO WAY" band veto to stop this after-band horrific-ness from happening.)

That evening I went to Cammy's house. She announced that all that was now left to do was for us to practise our autographs in case we were asked for them. This made me laugh. I didn't really think we'd be asked for them but it gave me a funny excited feeling in my tummy that we just MIGHT be, and also because this was REALLY happening (and that EDWARD was part of it).

And then I had one of the best ideas we'd had since we'd been coming up with best band ideas:

MARGARET'S PAWTOGRAPH!

I knew that people would obviously fall in LOVE with Margaret the minute they saw her in the band, so I suggested that we take lots of Margaret "pawtographs" with us and hand them out at the end of the gig.

Cammy thought it was a BRILLIANT idea too, and we started cutting out little squares of card and wrote "Margaret from The Spoons" at the top, in preparation for Margaret's paw prints.

However, getting Margaret's paw print was a little

more difficult than we'd thought it would be. We tried to use Nutella and jam, and managed to get as far as pressing her paw gently into the jam, but then she'd pull away and furiously lick her paw before we could press it down on the card. Then she would walk back over to us and happily let us dip her paw again only to fool us again by pulling it away at the speed of lightning and licking it clean.

After a couple of paws of each spread, Margaret decided she was going outside, and that was the end of the pawtographs. UNTIL … it started raining.

It scares me sometimes how our minds work. The SECOND Cammy and I heard rain hit the window we grabbed all the little pawtograph squares and ran downstairs to the kitchen and spread them out underneath the cat flap, making a sort of path out of the kitchen and into the hall (where we also put Margaret's food bowl).

Within a minute of doing so, Margaret came

rushing through her cat flap and quickly made her way along our "pawtograph path" all the way to her food bowl. RESULT!

We managed to get twenty-three really good pawtograph squares, which we were VERY pleased with. Go, MARGARET!

OUR FIRST LIVE GIG (PART 1)

Convincing Mum and Dad to give me a lift to the gig with Dad's old keyboard WITHOUT actually telling them what I was doing, or inviting them to stay, was tricky.

Mum, on usual "mum" form, asked 137 questions, each one more annoying than the last, and Dad wouldn't stop trying to talk to me about "keyboard stuff".

Sometimes people say that teenagers can be hard work. I feel I've heard that a lot. However, all I wanted on this occasion was to be driven to a semi-disclosed location, in silence, without fuss or questions, and to be picked up an hour and a half later. It might just be me, but I didn't think that sounded like hard work at all.

When we arrived at the venue, I was a bit surprised to see that it wasn't really a flashy new bowling alley (as I'd assumed it would be) but more of an old man's bowling clubhouse.

"Is this the right place, Peri?" said Mum.

"Yep," I replied, almost leaping out of the car.

Cammy was already there, waiting for me. I'd made her SWEAR she'd be there so that she could help me carry the keyboard inside (so no parental help was required!).

After asking Cammy twice if her mum was definitely inside waiting for us, my parents EVENTUALLY admitted defeat and reluctantly pulled away. Mum (of course) drove at a snail's pace, watching us the entire time until we went into the building and the door closed behind us. She is a NIGHTMARE!

It didn't really look like the type of place you'd expect to see a cool new band play. It looked much more like the type of place you'd expect to see old men drinking beer but I reminded myself that even the greatest bands had to start somewhere.

Cammy's mum was sitting at the bar with

Margaret, talking to an old (quite irritated-looking) man. She pointed at us when we walked in, and the man began making his way towards us.

"I'm Alf. You Edward's lot?" he asked.

"Erm, yes," I said.

"Through there," he said, pointing to a door at the back of the room. "Which one of you is the singer?"

That's when me and Cammy realised at the same time that we didn't actually HAVE a set lead singer. We all sang the words (when there WERE words – our music was often wordless).

The guy just rolled his eyes at us a bit and said, "Well, there's only one mic in the middle of the stage. Try not to move it, or anything else for that matter. Everything's set up and ready for the bingo at 8pm. What about that?" he added, pointing to my keyboard. "You need power for that?"

It took me a second to realise what he was asking me. "Oh. No," I said. "It's got batteries."

"Good," he said, and then he turned and walked off.

I suppose I'd have to get used to having all these band-support people around, asking us questions all the time, if we were going to keep doing gigs. But it was making me feel a bit nervous, especially since Cara and Edward weren't even here yet.

Me and Cammy made our way to the back of the room and opened the door to our venue. The first thing I noticed was the smell. It smelled of old-man aftershave and chips. There were no windows.

The next thing I noticed was the "stage". It was a smallish wooden box with a curtain hanging over it to separate the front stage from backstage.

"How EXCLUSIVE!" said Cammy. She clearly loved it. I wasn't so sure.

My nerves were really starting to get the better of me. I looked at my watch. We only had half an hour before the gig started, and Edward and Cara weren't even here yet!

Cammy could sense I was panicking so she forced me to meditate "backstage" with her. It REALLY didn't help. Every time I took a deep breath I almost choked on stale aftershave and chip-pan grease.

After what felt like an eternity of non-relaxing meditation, the door swung open and Cara came rushing in.

"I'm so sorry!" she said, sounding MEGA-flustered. "My debate ran over. I got here as fast as I could."

"No worries," said Cammy chirpily. "We're almost ready."

Almost ready? ALMOST READY? We hadn't even set up. And Edward wasn't even here yet!

"I think we should phone Edward," I said. "Does anyone have his number?"

Cammy shook her head and so did Cara. Great.

"Wait," said Cara, sounding optimistic. "I'll text my brother. He might have it. They're in Rubik's

Cube Club together."

I was a bit surprised to find out that there WAS a Rubik's Cube Club, and also that Edward was part of it.

Cara's brother texted back immediately with Edward's number, which was awesome (and also a little sad. It made me imagine him just sitting in his room most nights with a phone in one hand and a Rubik's Cube in the other).

Cara called Edward. No answer. I had a bad feeling.

Just then Alf popped his head round the door. "You're on in fifteen."

Oh God.

"Right," said Cammy. "We need to forget about Edward not being here for now and just focus on getting set up and getting Margaret prepared."

It didn't take long to get set up. Cara had the backing tracks ready on her laptop and we managed to find an extension cord for the speakers. We positioned the keyboard, bongos and Margaret's seat as close to the microphone as we could and then we went out to the bar to get Margaret.

"Are your mum and dad not coming?" Cammy's mum asked me.

"Erm. No. They can't make it," I lied.

Cammy got a weird look on her face. She didn't like me lying to her mum.

"Can we take Margaret backstage now?" Cammy asked.

"Of course," said Cammy's mum. "But please don't let her out of her carrier until she's wearing her kitty-lead."

It wasn't until we took Margaret out of her cat carrier backstage that we all realised how much she seemed to HATE her kitty-lead.

"Maybe we should just sit her on a table in her carrier," I suggested.

But Cammy said that would make her feel (and look) like a prisoner, and that our fans needed to see that she was there of her "own free will", otherwise someone might phone the RSPCA.

So we did everything we could to coax Margaret into letting us put the little lead on her and she EVENTUALLY agreed when Cara opened a bag of cheesy puffs and sprinkled some of the cheese-dust on the ground for her.

So we tied Margaret, very securely, to a table behind the curtain, and Cara said she'd leave plenty of cheesy-puff dust to keep her "entertained" while Cammy went to get a bowl of water and I went to the toilet for the fortieth time.

When I came out, I saw that people had begun to arrive and take seats near the stage.

I couldn't believe people had actually come! I mean, we'd put up LOADS of posters and everything, and Miss Carrigan had said that she would spread the word too, but I was still a bit shocked that people had come to hear us play.

There were a few people I didn't recognise sitting next to Cammy's mum, and then I saw a boy who looked about the same age as us with puffy red hair like Cara's. I realised that it must be her brother, and that he was sat with people who were probably her mum and dad too, and also that she must be a twin! I hadn't even known she had a brother, never mind a twin.

I looked over at the door to see if Edward was one of the people arriving, only to see that Cammy was standing at the entrance handing out PAIRS OF SOCKS to all the (very confused) people as they came in – I had CLEARLY used my band veto too soon!!!

I ducked behind the stage curtain to see if Edward was there yet. He wasn't.

Cammy appeared with Alf. "You're on in two," he said.

I couldn't believe it. We were about to go on and Edward still hadn't arrived!

"Text him again!" I almost screamed at Cara. The tension was getting to me BIG TIME.

Cara put down her spoons and called Edward.

"It's going straight to voicemail," she said, sounding a bit like she was going to cry.

"We're just going to have to go on without him," said Cammy. "There's nothing else we can do!" She grabbed both of my hands and squeezed them. "We can DO this, Peri. Do you hear me? We can DO this!"

And then she grabbed Cara's hand too and pulled us both out on to the stage.

OUR FIRST
LIVE GIG
(PART DEATH)

I can barely bring myself to tell you what happened next. It was that bad. No, it was that HORRENDOUS!

There we were on stage (without Edward) with a "crowd" of twenty to twenty-five people looking at us.

"HELLO!" boomed Cammy into the mic.

Several people screwed up their faces and some even covered their ears.

Oh no. The mic was on too loud. I searched around the room for Alf. Surely he'd hear it and turn it down?

"We are THE SPOONS!" Cammy continued to boom.

A few people started laughing and looking at each other.

I looked around to see who was in the crowd. To be honest with you, I'd really hoped that there would be a big spotlight shining on to the stage, preventing me from being able to see the faces in the crowd properly and allowing me to focus on my music.

But there was no spotlight. I could see all of the puzzled faces VERY clearly.

I spotted Miss Carrigan and a couple of people from our year, and then to my absolute HORROR I saw Jessica Clark (and quite a few other poopulars). They must've come to see Edward. Buckets! I should've realised she'd be here! Now I was a MILLION times more nervous than I'd been before. Jessica would be WILLING us to fail. And then all of sudden Cammy shouted, "FIVE, SIX, SEVEN, EIGHT!"

It had begun.

The horror had begun.

TRACK ONE

Cara went to do her solo first as planned but then realised she'd left her spoons backstage and rushed off to get them. So I went first instead and gave the WORST keyboard solo that could possibly be done on earth by a human. Then Cara did a totally terrible spoon solo, since she'd come back on stage with just ONE spoon. And then there was a HUGE pause after Cara had finished beating her single spoon against the side of a chair, because Edward was supposed to be next, but he wasn't here and Cammy hadn't YET realised that meant it was HER turn.

EVENTUALLY Cammy began her bongo solo, but it sounded weird, and she stopped abruptly after only a few seconds. So we were forced to go into track two after a short (applause-less) pause.

TRACK TWO

Cara looked stunned when she realised that she was going to have to do the whole song herself (with just ONE spoon). So I ran backstage to see if I could find the second spoon, only to find that Margaret was GONE!

I felt my heart drop to my feet.

I ran around backstage looking for her, but I couldn't find her anywhere.

TRACK THREE

I was seriously panicking that we'd lost Margaret, so I ran back on to the stage to tell Cammy at the exact moment that she tried to save the gig by playing her weird-sounding bongos just as the side of the bongos split open (never use cardboard to make bongos) and loads of SPOONS came pouring out on to the stage!

Cammy picked up the spoons and stared at them in disbelief.

And that's when I looked out into the crowd and saw a VERY angry face. It was the HEAD TEACHER!! What the FLAPJACK was *HE* doing here?!

He stared angrily back at me. Oh no. I thought back to what he had said in his office that terrible time: "*And what about the rest of the spoons?*"

Someone must have stolen more spoons from the cafeteria. THAT'S why the head was so angry about the two spoons on our notice. And that's when I realised we'd been SABOTAGED.

"Margaret's gone!" I blurted out in the middle of everything.

Cammy chucked the bongos to one side and ran backstage. As it hit the floor the second drum exploded and even MORE spoons fell out.

Cammy's mum ran backstage too. As we all searched for Margaret I heard Cara take the mic and say, "I'm sorry. It's over."

Everyone was silent except for a few kind-hearted/ tipsy people, who cheered.

"MARGARET! MARGARET!" Cammy screamed.

"THERE SHE IS!" I shouted. Thank God! Margaret had slipped her lead and was crammed inside a jumbo bag of cheese puffs, stuffing her face.

Cammy's mum scooped her up and said she was going

to take her home right away, and that she'd come back for Cammy when she'd finished getting her stuff together.

I could tell from her tone that she was less than pleased we'd almost lost Margaret, and probably even LESS pleased that Margaret had been eating "junk food" again.

Then Cara's mum and dad poked their heads backstage and said they'd wait for Cara in the car.

We all just kind of stood there staring at each other.

Before I even realised I was doing it, I was shouting at Cara. Saying that she had been in charge of ONE THING, which was to make sure Margaret had enough cheese-dust to keep her happy. Cammy was crying. And just then Edward came RUSHING in.

"I'm so sorry!" he panted, trying to catch his breath. "I fell off my bike and bust my phone. Have I missed it?"

Without answering, Cara stormed out and Cammy just stood there crying.

Edward looked at me, completely stunned, and said, "What happened?!"

SABOTAGE?
OR A NATURAL
DISASTER?

The next day in school wasn't great. I kept waiting for the head teacher to call me to his office about the spoons.

Cara had sent Cammy a text saying that she wouldn't be able to come to band practice for the rest of the week because she had loads on. Which we both knew was a lie, and that she wasn't coming because I'd shouted at her for losing Margaret.

Edward wasn't in that day, and I had no idea why, and I couldn't even text him to check that he was OK after his bike accident because he'd bust his phone. But worst of all Cammy was freaking out. She'd almost started crying in registration when a few people began drumming on their desks and laughing. Usually Cammy just ignores that kind of stuff and it's ME who gets bothered by it.

I explained to her that we'd clearly been SABOTAGED. And that it was most likely Jessica who'd tampered with Cammy's bongos when we were getting ready backstage. I was sure that Jessica and the poopulars must have stolen the rest of the spoons as a prank so that WE'D get the blame. Jessica clearly liked Edward and was probably jealous that he was hanging out with us all the time and decided to wreck our band because of it.

But Cammy said that she didn't think it WAS Jessica who had sabotaged us. She said that Jessica had been really nice to her after the gig, and had asked Cammy if she needed a lift home when she was stood outside waiting for her mum to come back to collect her.

I was actually stunned. Was Cammy being serious? Could she honestly not see that Jessica had set us up?

"Do you think the head's planning to expel us?" Cammy said, looking teary again.

"No," I said firmly. "I think it was pretty obvious that we didn't know the spoons were in there. If anything, he'll just ask to see me again."

Cammy put her head in her hands and said that we should probably just forget about the band. And even though last night had been AWFUL, I was still gutted when she said that, because I really didn't want The Spoons to break up.

Everything was sort of OK-ish by the end of the week. I'd decided to take the plunge and go to see the head myself; he SEEMED to believe what I told him about the sabotage (I did not mention Jessica by name, because Cammy made me promise I wouldn't).

I hadn't really seen Edward much, and he hadn't been able to come to the emergency band meeting that I'd scheduled to discuss "next steps" (neither had Cara, unsurprisingly).

I felt bad about shouting at Cara like I had. I knew it hadn't just been because she'd almost lost Margaret; I'd been jealous of how well she'd been getting on with Cammy (and how much she'd been encouraging Cammy's crazy ideas).

So anyway, Cammy and I decided to go ahead with the emergency meeting by ourselves. Cammy suggested that we take a break from rehearsals for a week or so. She also said that she was considering learning to play a more "normal" instrument for our comeback, like the "normal drums", since her bongos were ruined anyway.

I didn't mind at all that Cammy wanted to play the "normal drums" instead of the bongos, I was just relieved that she seemed to want to keep the band going (even if we just practised together for fun and never did a gig ever again!). But I did think it was a bit weird of Cammy not to WANT to play something weirder, like the harp.

The more I thought about it, Cammy had been acting a little less strangely since the disaster gig.

By the end of the day, I'd decided to make the effort to find Cara and apologise for shouting at her at the gig.

But I didn't have to, she found me! She was waiting for me at my locker at the end of sixth period.

"Oh. Hi!" I said. "I was actually looking for you."

Cara looked at me like she didn't really believe me.

And then she said, "You don't have to come. My mum and dad are making me invite everyone in our class." And then she handed me an invitation. "It's our annual Halloween bash," she said. "We always have one."

"Oh thanks," I managed to say through the awkwardness and guilt.

I was just trying to get the courage to make the situation even more uncomfortable by bringing up the shouting thing at the gig when Cammy appeared. She seemed to be in a much better mood.

"It's going to be the best Halloween party ever!" said Cammy. "We should all go as natural disasters!"

I'd started to protest at this "a step too far" idea. But I don't think anyone noticed because Cara had just shouted, "That's a FANTASTIC IDEA!" And now she was high-fiving Cammy loads.

NIGHT-VISION GOGGLES

LESSON — ALWAYS MAKE A "PROS AND CONS LIST" BEFORE DECIDING WHETHER OR NOT TO HELP YOUR GRAN DO SOMETHING A BIT BONKERS

By the time I'd walked home, I'd decided that Cara really didn't like me. She was clearly OBSESSED with Cammy and thought she was the best thing since, well, spoons, I suppose. She probably hadn't even been that bothered that I'd shouted at her.

Somewhere between watching Cammy and Cara become best friends and arriving home, I'd decided to go to the Halloween party as a moth. I don't really know why. I was in a moth kind of mood. But I figured that moths were pretty terrifying, with their weird cocoon-like bodies and their papery wings, so I thought it might make a good Halloween costume.

When Mum got home I went downstairs to ask her

if she could take me to Gran's so I could use her sewing machine (and by "use her sewing machine" I of course mean "get Gran to make it for me").

If ONLY I had known what was waiting for me at the bottom of the stairs, I would have locked my bedroom door and stayed in there for all time.

Mum had just bought a new PHONE.

I was forced into one of those awful conversations you have to have when an old person asks you to explain something electronic to them.

In my opinion, these situations never end well.

Background Information

My mum isn't really what you would call up to date with technology. One awful day she turned to me, and said:

"Peri, what's the Internet?"

(And please bear in mind that I am only twelve years old, so it's not like she asked me this fifty years ago or something when people were somehow managing to exist without going online!)

After about an hour, five arguments and a migraine, Mum eventually gave up and went back to her book. Thank God. I honestly don't know where she gets this "weird inability to understand anything normal" from. I mean, I'm pretty sure Dad had the old dial-up Internet in the house before I was even born! And Gran's a texting queen!

Awesome texts that I have received from my gran:

> HELLO SWEETHEART. HOW ARE YOU? MY LEGS ARE BAD TODAY. TOOK ME A CENTURY TO GET TO THE DOOR WHEN THAT NOSY WINDOW CLEANER RANG THE BELL. HE WAS LONG GONE BY THE TIME I GOT THERE. NOW I WON'T HAVE TO PAY. LOL ☺

> HELLO SWEETHEART. HOW ARE YOU? MY ARMS ARE BAD TODAY. DOORBELL WOKE ME UP AT 8AM. THOUGHT IT WAS THAT GREEDY WINDOW CLEANER AFTER MORE MONEY. IT WAS A PIZZA DELIVERY MAN. HE HAD A HUGE PIZZA. AS BIG AS A BUS. ASKED ME IF I ORDERED IT. I SAID, "OF COURSE NOT! DO I LOOK LIKE I EAT PIZZA FOR BREAKFAST?" AND THEN HE BACKED DOWN THE STEPS SLOWLY AND WENT AWAY. WHAT A SILLY MAN. OMG.

> HELLO SWEETHEART. HOW ARE YOU? I HAVE JUST LOOKED AT THE CLOCK ON THE COOKER AND REALISED THAT IT IS IN FACT 8PM, NOT 8AM. I AM GOING BACK TO BED NOW. I WILL PUT THE TOAST AND TEA I HAVE JUST MADE FOR MY BREAKFAST IN THE FRIDGE FOR TOMORROW. LOL ☺

So anyway, I tried to run back upstairs when I saw what was going on, but Mum caught me.

I did my best to protest by saying I wasn't feeling very well, and that maybe she should ask Dad to help her instead, but Dad was conveniently "busy".

So I went hunting for him and found him hiding behind the dishwasher, "fixing" it (which Mum has been asking him to do for ages). How interesting that he eventually decided to do it when Mum came back from town with a new phone.

Oh God. I can just imagine the state of the poor man in the phone shop. I bet he had to go home after she left.

In the end, Mum decided to retire to her room to "bond" with her new phone, so Dad said that he would drive me to Gran's.

Unlike Mum, Gran appears to know *exactly* what the Internet is, and in fact the minute Dad left she asked me if I could help her buy something online.

Night-vision goggles.

What do you say to that?

Pros & cons of helping my bonkers gran buy night-vision goggles

Pros

I will surely become the favourite granddaughter.

I will not have to have the really awkward conversation with her where I tell her "no".

She will be able to snoop on that "nosy witch" who lives across the road all night long if she wants. (I'm not sure if this is really a pro but I'm sure it would make Gran happy, so I'll add it anyway.)

She will save on electricity since she'll never watch the TV again.

cons
Dad could find out and I'd get into trouble for "encouraging" her.

Someone could phone the police to report "stalking."

Gran could get arrested.

Gran could go to prison, and who would make my moth costume then???

Fortunately for everyone, Gran nearly fainted when I told her how much night-vision goggles cost. (Gran still begrudges paying any more than 50p for shoes, and spends a lot of time in charity shops haggling with the kind volunteers over things like someone's old tights.)

It took a while to get her focused on making my

costume because she found out I hadn't had my dinner yet (even though it *was* only 5.30pm) and she started banging pots and pans about and calling Mum a "silly career woman". Then she forced about half a tonne of some sort of "stew" down my throat. But eventually she sat down at her sewing machine and made me a masterpiece!

SLAMMED BY MR PHART

LESSON — TRY NOT TO GET CAUGHT MAKING FUN OF TEACHERS (SOME OF THEM HAVE AN EVIL SIDE)

The next day at school I told Cammy about my moth costume.

"What about your face?" she said.

"What *about* my face?"

Note to reader: I am very paranoid about my face. It is quite large. In fact, I'm pretty sure I have enough face for at least two faces.

"I mean, are you going to wear a mask or something?" she said.

Due to my face-paranoia it took me several seconds to realise Cammy wasn't suggesting that I

236

wear a face-mask in general and that her question was moth-costume-related.

"I don't think I know what a moth's face looks like," I said.

So Cammy started doing some sketches in her workbook of what she thought a moth's face would look like. It looked brilliant! And hideous!

But then Mr Phart came *running* over.

"More sketches, I see!" he said.

Uh-oh. I just KNEW where this was going.

"And I assume this is a sketch of my face, *IS IT?*"

I *KNEW* he was going to think that we were drawing something to do with him again!

I was about to protest, and explain about the moth thing, but then I looked at Cammy's sketch and noticed that it really DID look a bit like Mr Phart. (Mr Phart is a very unfortunate-looking man.)

"It's not you, I promise!" said Cammy. "It's for

Peri's Halloween costume! She's going as a moth!"

A strange look passed across Mr Phart's face at this point.

I now know that this was the look of a man who had been wronged.

A man who had been wronged, and saw an opportunity to strike back with a vengeance!

"A *MOTH*?" he sneered.

And then he looked at the rest of the class and laughed.

"Well, I suppose you *do* look a bit like a creepy insect of some sort!"

And then the rest of the class burst out laughing too.

Did Mr Phart just call me creepy?

And an insect?

Is he allowed to do that??!

I couldn't believe it.

I'd been "slammed" by a teacher.

Slammed by MR PHART of *all* teachers!

The beast.

I watched as Mr Phart squeaked back over to his desk.

And then he "smiled" at me.

238

It was not a friendly smile.

It was the smug smile of someone who was clearly trying to convey a message:

PAYBACK.

"NO I'M NOT A DEAD OWL."

LESSON — IF YOU CAN'T KEEP A SECRET...LEARN!

On Thursday night I arrived late to Cara's party because Dad had been stuck in the toilet for ages (my life!).

When I eventually got there I couldn't believe how great the place looked. Cara's family had gone ALL OUT with the decorations. Their house looked super-creepy since it was really old and surrounded by dark fields. There were also about ten (brilliantly disturbing) zombies wandering around the garden as "decoration". It was awesome!

Dad looked freaked out when he saw them.

"You want me to stay here until you get in?" he asked as one of the zombies headed towards the car.

I had barely even said no when my freak of a dad basically pushed me out of the door and drove away before the zombie could touch him.

"Good costume. You're a dead owl, right?" said the zombie as he walked me up to the house.

"Erm, no. I'm a moth."

"Cool. Dead moth is good too," he said. "I'm Ziggy. Cara's brother."

"Oh yeah. You came to our gig," I said (and then wished I hadn't). He looked at me with zombie pity.

"Well, you guys can always join us tonight if you fancy it?" said Ziggy as he did a little dance. "We don't have a keyboard but you could try your hand at the spoons?"

I was about to ask him what he meant when Cara and Cammy appeared, joined at the hip (literally).

"What do you think?" beamed Cammy. "We're an EARTHQUAKE."

Cara looked mega-happy.

"Well, technically, I'm the aftershock," said Cammy.

"You look brilliant, Peri!" said Cara. "I'm so glad you came!"

"Thanks," I said. I was a little bit shocked at how happy Cara seemed that I'd come to her party. "I'm a—"

"You're a MOTH!" said Cara before I could finish. "You look fantastic! How did you make your mask?"

"Um. My gran made it. She used to mend costumes for the theatre."

Just then an army of (extremely non-scary) witches, cats and princesses walked past us and into the house (without even saying hello to Cara!).

"Was that the poopulars?" I asked Cara.

"Yeah," said Cara, seemingly unbothered by the fact that real-life demons had just entered her home.

"Come and see Cara's mum and dad!" squealed Cammy as she pulled me inside.

Cara's house looked even creepier on the inside than it did on the outside. There were zombies EVERYWHERE. Some were fake and some were real and you couldn't really tell which were which until one of them grabbed you. It was terrifying! (In a good way.)

"Most of the undead are my brother's friends from uni. They're fun," said Cara as one tried to strangle her.

"Mum! Dad!" Cara shouted across the room. "This is Peri."

I watched as two of the tallest people in the room made their way over. They looked TERRIFYING!

"Guess what they are, Peri!" said Cammy excitedly.

I couldn't stop staring at Cara's mum. She looked like she was on fire!

"They've come as natural disasters, too."

"Hello, Peri. I'm Eve, Cara's mum. And this is my husband, Ruirhi. We're a forest fire!"

"Wow!" I said. "You both look great." And they

really did! I'd been a little anxious to meet Cara's mum and dad, in case Cara had mentioned the me-shouting-in-her-face-and-blaming-her-for-everything thing. But they were really nice.

"It's almost TIIIIIMMMMMMEE!" one of the zombies announced. "Please gather in the barn if you DAAAAARE!"

Outside was a barn filled with haystacks and hanging lights and a mini STAGE!

Before I could even process what was happening Cara, her mum and dad, and her brothers got on stage and began playing some of the best (and quite weird) folk music I'd ever heard. There was a LOT of spoon action.

I looked around the room to see how everyone was responding. Most people were dancing and having a great time. Except for a crowd of princesses and witches, and a small colony of rabbits, who were pointing and sniggering at Cara and her family as if to say, "What are they DOING up there?"

And then I caught Jessica Clark's eye. She was standing next to the most ridiculous cat I have ever seen. I mean, if *MARGARET* tried to leave the house looking like that, I'd ask her to put some clothes on!

I looked away before she could turn me to stone. Cammy seemed to have disappeared. And then I spotted her at the front of the stage dancing like a maniac.

I suddenly felt quite uncomfortable with the poopulars standing at the back judging everyone, so I decided to look for somewhere to stand at the side until Cammy was finished her "I'm possessed" dance.

That's when I noticed a very odd-looking person at the side of the barn.

I looked closely at the odd-looking person. It was Edward!

He was dressed as, well, at the time I didn't really know *what* he was dressed as! His hair was slicked into the middle of his head and he had this weird granddad cardigan on.

But then I saw his feet.

On one foot he had an old greyish sock and a sandal, and on the other foot he had a shiny new shoe! It was HILARIOUS!

I was so impressed that I completely forgot about everything and went running straight over to him.

"You're Mr Phart! That's brilliant!" I said.

He looked at me a bit funny for a second.

"Oh, Peri. Hi! I didn't recognise you."

(That's when I remembered I had my mask on.)

I know I should have taken it off at this point, like you do with hats, to be polite. But I didn't. And I don't really know why. Our conversation therefore went a bit like this:

"So you like my costume then?" he asked.

"It's brilliant!"

"Sorry?"

He can't hear me. My mask is too heavy-duty and the music's too loud.

"IT'S BRILLIANT!"

I'm pleased I decided to keep my mask on since I just spat all over my face by mistake.

"Thanks. I thought you'd like it!"

"DO YOU LIKE ME?"

NO! OH MY GOD! That is NOT what I meant to say!!

"SORRY! NO! I MEANT TO SAY DO YOU LIKE MOTH? I MEAN, MY COSTUME?"

Aaaaaaarrrrrrggghhhhhh!!!!!!

I can feel my face burning under my mask. I'll probably set myself on fire in a minute. I can't BELIEVE what's happening!

He's not replying. He's just staring at me.

Just then everyone started clapping and cheering.

"Before our next song we'd like to announce the prize for the most TERRIFYING costume."

And then Cara and her brothers did a cool (spoons-only) drum roll for ages, gaining in speed until I thought their hands might fall off.

"And the winner is ... JESSICA CLARK!"

Everyone cheered, including the poopulars, as Jessica walked up to the stage to collect her prize.

Jessica was dressed as a BRIDE.

She looked confused as she shook Cara's dad's hand and accepted her prize.

She clearly hadn't intended to look terrifying.

As she stepped off the stage that's when Cara's dad said, "In some countries children are married as young as eleven years old. This is terrible and must be stopped. Thank you, Jessica, for choosing to raise awareness of such an important issue this evening."

And then everyone clapped loudly as Jessica and the poopulars just stood there, stunned.

"Wow," said Edward. "That was awkward!"

I burst out laughing. I couldn't help it.

And then Cara's dad said, "This one is for all the young hearts out there. Live and love, people. Live and love."

And then they started playing a SLOW SONG!

Note to reader: One of the reasons I hate school dances and parties is largely because of the whole "slow song" thing. It's horrible. The lights go down, and all the girls basically freeze on the spot and start panicking that nobody's going to ask them to dance. I tend to start panicking in case somebody actually *does* ask me to dance since I have NO IDEA how to do it.

Slow songs are pretty much a lose-lose situation for me. I mean, if someone *does* ask me, let's face it, it's probably going to be Max Martin. And as well as demonstrating my complete lack of coordination to the entire school, I will probably catch "unicorn-itis". However, if *nobody* asks me, then I'll be one of those girls left at the side, examining the sandwiches and generally trying to blend in with the buffet.

One of the major dangers of the slow song is that you can never quite time when it is going to ATTACK. Everyone knows it's a given that they're going to play one at the very end of the night (which is why Dad is under strict instructions to arrive no later than fifteen minutes before the end of each school dance) but there's *always* another one tucked in there somewhere that they release without warning at some random point during the night (so there's no time to run and hide in the toilets until it's over).

So I just stood there next to Edward while people began pairing up and wished that I was in my usual slow-song spot, next to the buffet with my friends (the sandwiches). I also wished I was a little less hairy, and a lot more invisible.

And then it happened.

Max Martin appeared and asked me to dance.

He was dressed as a frog. I do not know why.

I stood there frozen to the spot. How had he even recognised me?!

Before I could reply, Edward took my moth-hands

and said, "Sorry, Max, I just asked Peri to dance with me."

Thank God I had the mask on. Otherwise he would have seen me smile uncontrollably.

My head felt weird as we danced. Like I'd had ten Cokes and no sleep.

"Sorry, I hope you don't mind dancing with me," said Edward as we danced to my new favourite song of all time (who would have guessed I'd have my first dance with a boy to the sound of Cara playing the spoons?).

"No, it's great!" I said, too enthusiastically.

Once the song ended, we went to get some juice and sat down on one of the hay bales.

My legs felt weird and shaky, but in a good way. The juice helped a lot! As soon as I felt cooler I took my mask off and we chatted for ages. Edward was actually easy to talk to and I began to stop being so nervous around him and relaxed. It was going brilliantly. Edward was telling me all about how he learned to play the guitar, and how he used to live in Australia and before I knew it I was talking LOADS and answering his questions and we were chatting like we'd known each other all of our lives. But then something terrible happened.

Edward asked about me and Cammy and how we met and became best friends and before I even REALISED what I was saying, I told him about our first week at Fortress and the register, and Cammy's DEEP, DARK SECRET just slipped out!

I put my hand over my mouth in horror, and that's when I saw Cammy staring at me. She'd overheard everything.

And then she turned and ran, knocking the entire buffet table over as she left.

CAMEMBERT THE SMELLY CHEESE

LESSON — IF POSSIBLE TRY NOT TO HAVE ANY DEEP, DARK EMBARRASSING SECRETS — THIS WILL MAKE YOUR LIFE MUCH EASIER

The next day at school, word had spread about Cammy's dramatic departure. EVERYONE was talking about it.

And I couldn't find Cammy anywhere. I finally spotted her in the lunch queue and ran over.

"Oh my God, are you OK?"

"I'm fine."

"Seriously?"

"Yes."

It was obvious that Cammy wasn't really speaking to me.

This was awful. Poor Cammy. I was her BEST FRIEND and I'd gone and betrayed her trust and blabbed her secret to Edward.

"I'm so sorry, Cammy. I didn't mean to tell him."

I was terrified. I mean, I didn't know if she was going to forgive me or not. I was hoping she would and that she would also understand that it wasn't really my fault, and that it was all Mum's fault for passing on her talking disease to me.

I was just about to explain that her secret was still safe and that Edward wouldn't tell ANYONE when someone shouted, "EEEEErrrggghhhh! What's that STINK?!"

I turned round to see Jake Jones standing right behind us holding his nose.

"Can anyone else smell CHEESE?"

Everyone around us started giggling and whispering.

And Cammy gave me the worst look EVER.

Oh God. No. Edward must have BLABBED. And now Cammy was going to think it was ME!

"That's your *real* name isn't it, Cammy?" said Jake. "CAMEMBERT THE SMELLY CHEESE!"

I could feel my heart racing.

Cammy put down her tray and walked out.

How could Edward do this to Cammy? To *ME*?

I turned and saw that Jessica was looking right at me. She was smiling.

I couldn't believe that Edward had told someone. Possibly even Jessica. He'd promised not to tell! And now the poopulars knew! What a vom-face. I was never going to talk to him EVER again. This was ALL his fault.

❧

That night I phoned Cammy like a MILLION times, but she wouldn't pick up her phone. She was probably in her mum's crystal room, lying on the massage bed surrounded by candles and soothing music.

I was just about to ask Mum if I could go over to her house when my phone beeped:

HELLO PERI. JESSICA HAD A WORD WITH ME AFTER SCHOOL. SHE TOLD ME EVERYTHING. I KNOW THAT YOU'RE THE ONE WHO TOLD MY SECRET TO EVERYONE. HOW COULD YOU?! JESSICA SAID THAT YOU TOLD HER AT CARA'S PARTY AND THAT YOU'VE BEEN LAUGHING ABOUT ME BEHIND MY BACK. SHE ALSO SAID THAT YOU DIDN'T GO TO THE HAIRDRESSERS THAT DAY AT BAND PRACTICE, AND THAT YOU WERE OFF AUDITIONING FOR ANOTHER BAND!!! AND I KNOW IT'S

TRUE PERI BECAUSE YOUR HAIR DIDN'T EVEN LOOK DIFFERENT THE NEXT DAY! I HOPE YOU'VE ENJOYED MAKING FUN OF ME. YOUR FRIENDSHIP WITH BOTH ME AND MARGARET IS OVER.

I couldn't believe it! I couldn't BELIEVE IT!

WHAT WAS HAPPENING??!!

I didn't know WHAT was going on. Why would Edward blab Cammy's secret? Especially to JESSICA! And WHY would Cammy believe it?!

I wasn't surprised that Jessica had got involved and was trying to turn Cammy against me. She'd obviously seen me dancing with Edward at Cara's party and was fuming with jealousy.

It was right there and then that I decided there was NO WAY I was going to let Jessica get away with making up lies and turning Cammy against me. NO WAY!

255

**EDWARD =
SNAKE
SNOT**

I texted Cammy and explained what had *really* happened, but she didn't reply. And when I tried to call her, her phone was switched off.

I lay on my bed, miserable, thinking about all the times Edward had obviously only been talking to me in the first place and acting all "human" and "awesome-like" so that he could gain my trust,

find out all my secrets and broadcast them to the world!

And then ANOTHER realisation popped into my head. Our GIG! It had been EDWARD who had set it up. EDWARD who had picked the rubbish venue. Oh God. It might have even been EDWARD who STOLE THE SPOONS and put them in Cammy's BONGOS.

And I bet he never fell off his bike! I mean, his hair wasn't even a mess when he turned up. What if he just joined our band and then didn't turn up for our first gig because he *wanted* to sabotage us, and wreck our band. Maybe he was one of them after all. A poopular!

I wondered if he'd actually been at the gig the whole time, watching and laughing, until it was all over. And then I realised that he and Jessica must've KNOWN the head teacher would be there, and that's why they picked such a weird place for our first gig, because THEY had been the ones to steal the spoons, and THEY wanted to frame US for it!

It was unbelievable! I wondered if that's what they had been plotting when I'd seen them in the library at Parents' Evening.

I couldn't wait to tell Cammy all of this tomorrow in registration. There was NO WAY she wouldn't be able to believe me with THIS much evidence.

VOODOO DOLL

LESSON – IT IS NEVER A GOOD SIGN IF YOU CATCH YOUR BEST FRIEND MAKING A VOODOO DOLL OF YOU

The next day at school, Cammy was back. She completely and utterly IGNORED me in registration, and when I tried to just tell her everything anyway, she asked Mr Burton if she could move seats.

I had no idea how I was going to get her to listen to me about what was really going on. I HATED not being able to speak to my own best friend.

I tried to talk to her again in Food Technology, but she just ignored me and continued to make what I'm pretty sure was a "Peri voodoo doll".

After class, I almost fainted with shock when *Edward* tried to talk to me! Can you believe it?! What a snake-snot. I just stopped dead and gave him a "look". I think he got the message.

The "Look"

Eyes
Screwed up, almost shut, with only a tiny sliver of eyeball visible.

Lips
Pulled perfectly into a deep snarl.

Ears
Well … I can't really move my ears, but in my mind they were pinned back the way Margaret's ears get when she's angry.

It seemed to work.

At lunch, Cammy was nowhere to be seen.

So I took my tray and sat down at an empty table, and prayed that Max Martin wouldn't take this as an open invitation to come and sit with me.

But I couldn't really eat anything because my stomach was hurting, and had been since the night before. I was also put off my food by the disgusting sight of Jessica sitting at the poopular table, probably coming up with more evil plans to ruin people's lives. I took pleasure in imagining she was munching cat-poo satay sprinkled with dinner-lady sneeze.

Then later, during Miss Morgan's class, Edward tried to talk to me AGAIN! But I just looked away and ignored him completely.

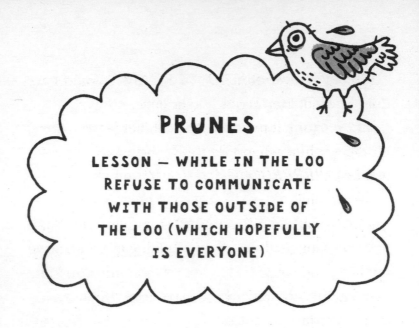

PRUNES

LESSON – WHILE IN THE LOO REFUSE TO COMMUNICATE WITH THOSE OUTSIDE OF THE LOO (WHICH HOPEFULLY IS EVERYONE)

After school, I just sat in my room and thought about the horrific-ness that was my life.

My best friend had made a voodoo doll of me, I was banned from seeing Margaret, and Mum and Dad were probably sitting downstairs right now flicking through *Every Parent's Guide to Total Offspring Humiliation – Part 2* for inspiration. Oh … and the boy I'd *liked* was a complete snail-trail.

I realised that all of this might be the reason my stomach was hurting so much (it also crossed my mind that this could be the work of Cammy's voodoo doll).

I decided to ask Mum for help. That was a grave mistake. Mum dragged me to the doctor's right away.

On top of everything else, I REALLY could have done without this terrible experience:

The doctor felt my stomach with her jaggy fingers.

"Does it hurt when I do this?" she asked.

AAAAARRRRRGGGGHHHHHH!

"Yes, a bit."

The brutal knife-fingered doctor then told Mum that she thought I was constipated (can you believe my life?) and wrote me a prescription for something that would "loosen my bowels" and "significantly reduce the faecal compaction".

Lovely.

I just wanted to get out of there and go home for a lie-down, but then Mum made us stop at the supermarket to buy prunes. She also got some prune juice, some herbal tea and a bag of figs. Apparently (in her non-expert opinion) these most disgusting fruits were the answer to all my tummy troubles.

After the concoction Mum made me eat/drink, I spent the rest of the night in the bathroom.

Dad had to drive back to the supermarket to use the toilet there.

I was humiliated.

My dad took this decision after what I believe to be

the worst conversation that I have ever had with him (or possibly any human being).

It went like this (if you can bear to read it):

"Are you going to be long in there?"

"Yes."

"Do I have time to finish my tea first?"

"Yes."

Five minutes later.

"Are you almost done in there?"

"No."

"Can you give me an idea of how long you'll be?"

"No."

"It's just I think that curry your mum made was a bit on the spicy side for me."

Please stop talking.

Enter Mum.

"What are you two saying about my curry?!"

"Nothing, love."

"So, do you think you'll be out soon, Peri?"

"NO."

"Steve, leave her be. Her bowels have loosened!"

Kill me. Kill me now.

"Peri, darling, would you like me to bring you a cup of herbal tea? Or maybe some more prunes?"

Oh God. No. No more prunes.

"No, Mum. I'm fine."

"Are you sure?"

"Yes. Wonderful. Just not in a very chatty mood right now."

"Well, there's no need to be cheeky!"

Seriously? Surely there is.

"Well, I guess I'll just have to drive round to Tesco and use the toilet there then?"

Was that a question?

Is my father trying to guilt me into coming out?

What does he think I'm doing in here? Reading War and Peace? *Holding the dog hostage? Having a PARTY?!*

The phone rings.

"Hello, Peri's slave speaking."

If I ever get off this toilet, I swear I'm phoning Childline.

"Erm … no. She's a bit … busy at the moment."

Oh no…

"She's been very ill, you know."

OH NO.

"I had to take her to the doctor's…"

Oh my God. Did she just say FAECAL COMPACTION?!

"I think it's all that cheese she eats."

PUT THE PHONE DOWN! PUT IT DOWN NOW!!

265

Once I eventually left the bathroom, I found out that it had been EDWARD who had phoned.

I was humiliated.

I mean, even though I *obviously* didn't like him any more (and in fact probably HATED him) I was still mortified that he had been involved in a conversation with my mother. A conversation with my *mother* about my *bowels*.

And how did he even get my phone number anyway? I mean, do people even still call landlines these days?

And why exactly was Edward "stalking" me now?

I was considering how to best report Edward's "stalker-ish" behaviour to the police when a TERRIBLE thought entered my head.

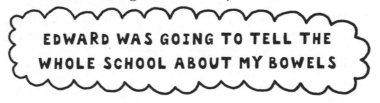

EDWARD WAS GOING TO TELL THE WHOLE SCHOOL ABOUT MY BOWELS

So this is when I decided to lock myself in my wardrobe and start writing my memoirs (since I was concerned that I might actually die of embarrassment when I go back to school on Monday and wanted to leave something of significance behind.)

And here I am.

I've been in here for most of the weekend.

Because life can't get much worse.

Note to self: I MUST remember to stop staying that! I KNOW it only makes things worse when I say "things can't get much worse!"

THE BOY TALK

LESSON - PARENTS TRY TO "TALK" WITH THEIR CHILDREN. KEEP MONEY, A COAT AND AN ENERGY DRINK WITH YOU AT ALL TIMES. YOU MIGHT HAVE TO GO INTO HIDING.

I eventually came out of my wardrobe today. I knew I had to face Fortress sometime! Before I left for school, my dad tried to talk to me about "boys". It was like death.

Like I didn't have enough stressing me out at the moment without adding Dad's "Boy Talk" to the mix! I mean, I'd spent the weekend in a wardrobe, my best friend had cursed my stomach and I was about to return to Fortress and have to deal with the inevitable "poo" jokes that awaited me (thanks to Mum).

But Dad WOULD NOT let the "boy" thing go.

Note to the world: I think it's weird that a word that is so normal and not at all weird can float around, not harming (or embarrassing) you for most of your life … until your DAD gets hold of it!

Examples of Acceptable Uses of the Word "Boys"

Cammy:
Those "boys" in Science class are evil worm-killers.

Miss Morgan:
It's time for the "boys" to start sharing their feelings with the talking stick.

Mum:
Those "boys" across the road look like vandals.

So why is it that when my dad uses this perfectly normal word it makes me feel like my skin is going to slide off?

Please observe the following terrible encounter:

"So…" says Dad as he mutes the TV.

That "so" sounded a little too chirpy for my liking.

"So?" I reply.

My "so" is delivered with a clear message of suspicion and general "please-don't-say-whatever-you-are-about-to-say-ness".

Dad turns the TV off.

This can't be good.

"How's … everything?"

I am finding it difficult to judge this situation. He's smiling, but he clearly doesn't *mean* it. Dad's an eye-smiler. And his eyes aren't smiling.

Oh! Maybe it's just my "tummy troubles". Maybe that's why he's being so weird.

"My stomach's fine now, Dad."

"Oh. Good. Yes. But how's everything else going?"

He's fake-smiling even more now.

Mum has clearly put him up to this. She's probably behind the couch. I bet she doesn't even have a job. I bet she just lurks around, constantly looking for opportunities to strike.

"Dad, what's going on?"

"Nothing's going on! Why would something be going on? Isn't a father allowed to ask his only daughter how she's getting on?"

No.

"Yes, I suppose so."

"So, how's everything at school?"

"Fine."

"And with Cammy?"

How does HE know about what happened with Cammy?

"Fine."

"GREAT!" he practically screamed.

That was a bit too enthusiastic.

Oh God. His eyes are really wide now.

I have NO IDEA what's going on.

"Oh. Yes. I almost forgot…"

No you didn't.

Here it comes.

Whatever it is.

"Your mum said a *boy* called, yes? Now, what was his name again?"

Like he'd EVER forget.

"Edward."

"Oh yes! That's it, Edward. Nice name. Sounds a bit old though. Is he? Is he old? He's not eighteen or something? He's not eighteen, is he?! No, I'm sure he's not. He's at school with you, isn't he? Is he in the same year? He's not older than you, is he? He's not a sixth-former or anything? No? No, I'm sure he's not. Why would a sixth-former be phoning you? That doesn't make any sense, does it? Ha, ha, silly Dad. So how is *Edward*? Did he say how he was on the phone? Mum said he sounded good. Is he good? Are you in the same class or something? Was he just calling about homework? Yes, he probably was, wasn't he?"

Wow.

How many questions was that?

This is the weirdest I have EVER seen Dad.

Even weirder than the time Mum tried to go topless in France.

"Dad, are you OK?"

"What? YES! Of course I am! Why wouldn't I be OK? Are you OK? You *are* OK, aren't you? You'd tell me if you weren't OK, wouldn't you?"

"I'm fine, Dad. Do you want a glass of water or something?"

"No thanks. So, tell me about this *boy*, *Edward*."

Oh God.

He's not giving up.

"Is he a nice *boy*?"

Err, NO!!!

"He's fine."

"Was he just phoning to *chat*?"

Dad almost choked on that last word.

"No. I don't know why he was phoning, actually."

"What?! Is this *boy* harassing you or something?!"

Please stop saying "boy".

"No, Dad. He was probably just phoning about homework or something, like you said."

I feel a bit bad lying to him, but if I tell him the truth I think he might actually behead Edward. Which is fine by me, I just don't want Dad going to jail, because there is NO WAY I could deal with Mum on my own.

"Oh. Yes. So … is this *boy* Edward your …"

Oh God. Please don't say it. Please, please pleeease!

"… *boyfriend*?"

He just used the "b" word AGAIN.

I have actually died of embarrassment.

"No. Definitely not, Dad."

"I see."

He clearly doesn't believe me.

"If he *IS* your *boyfriend,* you can tell us, you know?"

Us? Mum IS hiding behind the couch, isn't she?!

"He's not."

This is torture. He is actually torturing me.

"OK. Well, maybe we should have a little talk about *boys* soon anyway. Especially after that whole 'unicorn-fiasco'."

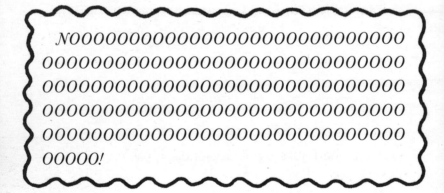

NOOOOOOOOOOOOOOOOOOOOOOOOOOOOOO OOOOOOOOOOOOOOOOOOOOOOOOOOOOOOO OOOOOOOOOOOOOOOOOOOOOOOOOOOOOOO OOOOOOOOOOOOOOOOOOOOOOOOOOOOOOO OOOOOOOOOOOOOOOOOOOOOOOOOOOOOOO OOOOO!

WHEN LIFE GIVES YOU LEMONS, CRUSH THOSE LEMONS, CHUCK THEM OVER THE FENCE AND MAKE AN AWESOME PLAN.

When I EVENTUALLY got to school, something bizarre was going on. Nobody was talking about my tummy troubles OR shouting "poo" jokes at me. It was weird.

Then during morning break, I found out why. My bowels were clearly old news because Cammy had just been crowned UGLY PIGEON!

I stood there (probably with my mouth hanging wide open) as everyone laughed and pointed at Cammy's locker. It had a huge U.P. sign drawn on it and horrible fake feathers taped everywhere. Jessica

was one of the people laughing too.

I ran over, actually grabbed Jessica by the arm and said, "You are literally the WORST human being I have EVER MET. Your mother must be ASHAMED!"

I was so shocked by what I'd done and what I'd said. I was absolutely furious, and I could feel my whole body shaking. Jessica looked shocked (she was probably scared in case I decided to bite her or something). I dropped her arm and turned to look at Cammy, but she was running down the corridor.

I ran, full-force, after her and eventually caught up with her outside our music cupboard.

"Cammy! Are you OK?" I said, putting my hand on her shoulder.

She spun round. She looked absolutely furious.

"No, Peri, I'm NOT OK. This is ALL your fault!"

"Cammy, please listen, it wasn't ME! Yes, I told Edward about your real name but it was by COMPLETE accident. You have to believe me, Cammy! I had no IDEA that he was going to blab it to other people and that Jessica would find out. It was Jessica, she set us all up. I think Edward's in on it too! They're proper EVIL, Cammy!"

Cammy just stood there, still looking furious, and that's when Miss Carrigan appeared and ushered us into the music cupboard.

"*Girls*, what on earth is going on? Are you OK?"

Cammy slumped down on one of the chairs and started crying.

So I told Miss Carrigan about what Jessica had done to Cammy's locker, and she sat with us for a while to make sure we were OK before going off to see the locker for herself.

Once Miss Carrigan was gone, I began explaining everything to Cammy.

I said I thought Edward *hadn't* fallen off his bike and that he'd not turned up to the gig on *purpose*, because he'd been in on Jessica's plan to sabotage our band. And that Edward had been the one who organised the bowling club for our gig because he knew the head teacher went there, and that they had stolen the spoons and framed us for it in front of the head (since we were called The Spoons).

Cammy just sat there and listened to everything, and she didn't interrupt me once.

When I was finished I expected her to say, "I can't believe this!" or "Peri, I'm so sorry!" and give me a hug or something, but she didn't.

She started blaming ME!

"This is still YOUR fault, Peri!" she started shouting. "Even if it was an accident, YOU'RE still the one who told Edward!"

Before I could reply, she stormed right out of the music cupboard and ran down the corridor.

I didn't go looking for Cammy after that, I just went to class. My head was spinning and I had no idea what to do or what I'd actually say to Cammy if I saw her.

By the end of English I'd decided that I was going to win Cammy back. I had a plan. I was going to make it up to Cammy and it was going to be AWESOME!

OPERATION AWESOME PLAN!

THE PLAN!

STAGE 1 - Cara

Even though Cammy hadn't said it, I knew myself that I'd treated Cara badly. I'd become jealous when I'd seen her and Cammy getting close.

So I texted Cara and asked if I could meet with her that night. Cara texted back right away saying that she was at a debating competition in the assembly hall and that she couldn't meet me.

So I packed up my stuff and went down to the assembly hall to see if I could speak to her there for a minute.

When I arrived, I spotted Cara up on stage. There were loads of people sitting down watching, and then someone announced that the debate was just about to start. So I sat down and watched. I'd never seen a debate before. It was pretty interesting actually!

When it was Cara's turn to speak, she absolutely SMASHED the competition. It was awesome! Every time the other girl gave an argument in favour of capital punishment, Cara waited until she'd finished and then absolutely wiped the floor with her!

I stayed and watched the whole thing, and I'm glad I did because Cara's team won the championship trophy!

I waited around at the end, and managed to get Cara's attention before she left with her family.

"What are *you* doing here?" she asked, looking mega-surprised to see me.

"I came to say sorry," I said. "I shouldn't have shouted at you like that after the gig. It wasn't your fault Margaret got away. I mean, even if it had been your fault, I still shouldn't have spoken to you like that. I'm sorry."

Cara looked surprised. She clearly hadn't been expecting that.

"Why are you apologising now?" she asked. "Is it because of what happened to Cammy?"

So I asked Cara if we could please meet tomorrow in the music cupboard at break so I could explain everything that had happened, and she agreed.

"You were AWESOME by the way!" I told her before she left. "I had no idea you could do that!"

"I know," she said, and smiled loads. "See you tomorrow."

A BADGE WITH MARGARET'S FACE ON IT WILL FIX EVERYTHING

The next day, once I'd explained everything to Cara, she said that she forgave me for shouting at her.

Cara said that she could tell that I didn't want her there, and that I didn't really like her, and that she'd felt that way since the day of the spoon audition when I hadn't looked very happy to have her join the band (which made me feel awful).

I explained to Cara that I DID like her (and I DID!) and that I'd just been stupid and jealous, and that I really wanted to keep getting to know her and be friends.

"Good!" said Cara. "Because I think you'll find I'm sort of awesome." And then she laughed and hugged me, and I was MEGA-relieved!

Stage 2 - Re-form the spoons.

Between the two of us, we absolutely perfected Stage 2 of my plan to make Cammy happy and get her to be my best friend again. And in a couple of days, we managed to:

1 Find Cara's missing spoon at the bowling club (I hadn't realised that they were special playing-spoons she'd ordered from Bulgaria for the gig).

2 Practise LOADS.

3 Get awesome badges made with Margaret's face on them (Cara managed to use her debating skills to get the guy in the shop to make loads of them for us FREE! She'd kept on saying stuff about "Big businesses showing their support for youths and the arts". It was brilliant!)

4 Get a gig at an actual REAL music venue!!!

In just a few days I'd MEGA-improved on the keyboard, thanks to my dad (surprisingly!). He'd come into my room while Cara and I were practising to see what I was up to and, as it turns out, Dad is actually kind of awesome on the keyboard, and he loves all the effects like I do. He even showed me how to use the laptop to "layer" music, which meant that I could record stuff and then play it back while I played more stuff over it – it sounded amazing!

Then me and Cara had the BESSSSSSSSST idea. We could RECORD Margaret and then play it as a kind of backing track while we all played so that Margaret could be part of the band without actually having to be there (because we were pretty sure Cammy's mum wouldn't let us take her to any more gigs).

Dad said that he'd come along if we wanted, and do all the sound engineering, and link up the laptop, and make sure there were enough mics, and check that the lights were right, etc. I didn't even know he could do all that, but he said that he used to do it all the time when he played keyboard in a band years ago.

Then he started telling us about that for ages and I had to try REALLY hard not to ask him to leave because he'd been speaking for almost half an hour.

Miss Carrigan was the one who managed to get us the great gig, in a REAL music venue that

LOADS of people go to. She'd been even more supportive of our band since the whole Ugly Pigeon thing. She even let us use the Music department's photocopier to make loads of flyers (when Mr Fry had gone home!).

A few days before the gig, there were only a couple of things we still had to sort out.

1. We hadn't finished making new bongos for Cammy (it was really hard!).
2. We had to get her to rejoin the band!

Cara said that she'd tried to speak to Cammy a few times that week, but Cammy hadn't been at school much since everything that had happened on Monday.

So the night before the gig, Cara said that it would probably be best if she was the one to speak to Cammy, so she arranged to go over to Cammy's house.

That night I was getting ready for bed when my mobile beeped. It was Cara. And all it said was:

SHE'S IN ☺

I literally started jumping up and down with happiness when I read it.

Within seconds both my mum and dad were at my bedroom door asking me if I was OK and trying to stop my wardrobe from toppling over.

I grabbed them both and gave them a big hug (which I realised I probably hadn't done for months).

"I'm fine!" I said (still jumping up and down). "I'm just really excited about our gig on Saturday! Mum, will you come too?" I said before I'd even realised it.

And that's when Mum started crying (in a good way).

THE
SPOONS
REUNITED

On Saturday me and Dad were all packed up, sitting in the living room waiting for Mum to get back from the shops so we could leave for the gig.

"Dad, where *is* she?" I asked, getting nervous. I was dying to get to the gig and see Cammy, and really worried that we weren't going to have enough time to set up.

"Don't worry," said Dad. "We've still got plenty of time." But then he kept looking at his watch so I didn't really believe him.

Just then Mum literally BURST through the door with a big shopping bag.

"I got something for you!" she gasped.

I was ready to scream because Mum had obviously picked me up some horrendous outfit and was happily making me late for the gig while she went shopping for nonsense that she should have KNOWN I would never wear!

"Mum, please! Can we just go?"

And that was when Mum pulled a brand-new set of bongo drums out of the bag.

"I had to drive out of town to get them," she said. "I hope they're OK."

I couldn't believe it. Cammy would be thrilled!

When we arrived at the venue, Cammy wasn't there yet.

Cara had made a little bow for the bongos out of paper, and we hid them backstage for Cammy.

Dad got to work setting everything up and doing the soundcheck, while me and Cara practised backstage.

"WOW!" I heard a wonderful voice say. "Are these for me?"

I turned to see Cammy standing with her new bongos.

"Yes," said Cara. "Otherwise you'd have had to use these!" She held up the pair we'd tried to make and laughed.

"My mum got them for you," I said.

"Wow, that was really nice of her," said Cammy.

Then Cara muttered something about needing to fetch her laptop, and disappeared out the front.

"Look who I brought…" Cammy said, and then she went back behind the curtain and brought Margaret in on her lead.

"I've been training her," said Cammy. "Haven't I, Margaret?"

Margaret meowed just like she always does when Cammy asks her a question.

Then Cara came back in with her laptop and said, "Listen," and that's when I heard LOADS of Margaret's sounds.

"We recorded them last night at Cammy's," said Cara. "I'm working on them with your dad now." And then she disappeared again.

There was an awkward silence for a bit.

"I'm sorry," said Cammy. "I shouldn't have got so cross with you."

I shook my head. "Cammy, I honestly didn't mean to blurt your darkest secret out. I was being an idiot, trying to impress a stupid boy, but I'm back to my normal self now, I promise! I'm never going to think about Edward Snail-Trail ever again."

Cammy smiled.

"Well, you MIGHT have to think just a little bit about him."

And then she pointed behind me, and I saw that he was walking towards me. The Snake-Snot Master himself.

"Just listen to him, Peri," said Cammy, and then she gave me a big hug and left me there in complete bewilderment.

"OK, you need to get away from me," I managed to say before Edward actually dropped to his knees and looked like he was going to cry.

"Peri, I'm begging you! Look, I'm actually begging you! I didn't tell ANYONE about Cammy's real name. Jessica overheard our conversation. SHE'S the one who told everyone. You have to believe me!"

I suppose that did seem a whole lot more likely.

"Cammy told me that you thought I'd been trying to wreck the band. I promise I didn't steal the spoons. I DEFINITELY didn't put them in Cammy's bongos and I had NO IDEA the head would be at the gig!"

I watched as he stood up and started to struggle with his trouser leg.

"And I honestly fell off my bike," he said. "Look!" And then he pulled up his trouser leg and there was a massive scabby scar with stitches that went right up his leg and over his knee.

"I had to go to A&E and everything, but I didn't want to make a big deal because Cammy was crying when I turned up and I felt bad for letting you guys down. And by the look on your face, you were a bit mad at me.

"Do you believe me, Peri?"

I stared at him for a while. I knew he was telling the truth.

"I believe you," I said.

"So you're not going to get your boyfriend, Max, to beat me up then? I've genuinely been very concerned about that," he said, smiling.

"Max Martin is NOT my boyfriend," I said

(hopefully for the last time ever!).

Edward grinned. "You sure?"

"Very," I said.

He went back down on his knees again, even though it must've really hurt.

"Petunia Perry ..." he said, and I burst out laughing because it looked like he was about to propose.

"... can I be a Spoon again?"

MARGARET'S BIG SURPRISE!

The gig was an AMAZING success. Sure, there were a few glitches. Like when no one remembered the words and Dad plunged the entire venue into darkness for over thirty seconds.

Actually, I think that one worked in our favour, because Cammy started doing a really cool, kind of creepy bongo solo and Margaret began wailing (she likes the dark). Then just as we all joined in, the lights came back on, which kind of made it look like it was on purpose. (And would have been 100% awesome rather than 95% awesome if Max Martin hadn't been audibly weeping because he's scared of the dark.)

Margaret, hands down, gave the best performance of her life. At the end of the last song, she started making all SORTS of noises we'd never heard before.

But then even after we finished playing and were packing up, Margaret wouldn't stop wailing. So me, Cara and Edward all went back to Cammy's with her mum, to make sure Margaret was OK. Me and Cammy thought that she was maybe having one of her "psychic migraines" but when we were in the car Margaret began yowling a LOT so Cammy's mum pulled over and called the 24-hour vet (and a couple of other people) and within minutes of getting home, the vet, Cammy's mum's spiritualist and someone with a LOT of candles turned up.

As soon as the vet began examining Margaret he said that she was in labour. We were all STUNNED. We didn't even know she was PREGNANT!

The vet kept saying that he couldn't understand how the other vet Margaret had been taken to a couple of weeks ago could have missed it.

"There's definitely a full litter in there," he said as he touched Margaret's tummy.

Cammy's mum said that she'd noticed Margaret had got a bit of a tummy lately, but had just thought it was because people (and she meant me, Cammy and Cara) had been feeding her junk food.

The vet said that Margaret needed peace and quiet (which made me feel TERRIBLE because she'd just been to a rock concert!). So I phoned Mum and she came and picked us all up.

We all chatted to Mum about the gig, but mostly about Margaret the whole way to Edward's house. And when Edward got out, he squeezed my hand a bit, but no one else noticed except for me. It was amazing.

LIFE AIN'T SO BAD WHEN THERE'S JUSTICE AND A BABY PIGEON IN THE WORLD!

The next day at school, Cammy came RACING into registration.

"I've been up all night!" she screamed. "Margaret's had QUINTS!"

Mr Burton immediately assumed Cammy was talking about a person giving birth to five babies and he looked totally shocked.

Once we'd set him straight, Mr Burton (who happens to be a cat person) got quite excited and asked if she had any pictures. Cammy (of course) had about five hundred photos of the kittens on her phone.

Mr Burton managed to connect Cammy's phone

to the projector and we showed them to the whole of our registration class. Even the poopular girls at the back loved them, and EVERYONE was asking Cammy if they could have one!

At one point Cammy pointed to the littlest, tiniest one and said that she'd called it Pigeon, and everyone laughed, and I knew right away that I had to have it (if Cammy and my mum would let me!).

And then all of a sudden Miss Carrigan turned up at the door with Jessica Clark and asked to see Cammy outside.

I started to worry that Jessica had maybe accused Cammy of doing something to her, but Cammy came back in after a few minutes and sat down.

"What was THAT?" I asked.

"Jessica just apologised to me for what she did to my locker. Miss Carrigan's taking her to see the head now," she said.

Wow. I hadn't realised just how good a teacher Miss Carrigan was. She must've had to quiz Jessica for HOURS to eventually get a confession out of her!

I tried to imagine Jessica apologising to Cammy outside.

"Do you think she really is sorry?" I asked Cammy. She hadn't looked very sorry when I'd seen her at the door. She'd looked more annoyed.

"No, not really, but I don't care," she said. Just then Mr Burton flicked to the next picture and Cammy started telling everyone what this kitten was called and why.

I smiled. Cammy was right. Who cared about stupid Jessica Clark?

Then suddenly the picture of the kitten disappeared and was replaced with a video.

At first I didn't know what I was looking at, and then I realised it was the school cafeteria. "This isn't mine!" said Cammy. "My phone doesn't do videos!"

We all stared at the screen, watching as Jessica stuffed loads of spoons into her school bag. I couldn't believe it!

Mr Burton furiously tapped all the keys on his keyboard, but nothing would make it go off. The video was on a loop!

Then the bell went and we heard EVERYONE in the corridor talking about it.

When we went out we saw that it was also playing on the big info screens all the way along the corridor too!

"Oh my God, Cammy! Is it playing on every screen in the school?" I asked, stunned at what was happening.

I couldn't figure out who had done this!

Cammy pulled me to one side and handed me a note.

"I found this in my locker last week. I didn't know what it meant at the time, but…"

I unfolded it and read:

Dear C

The Hacker would like you to know that he is in NO WAY responsible for leaking the information about your real name. He wants you to know that he will fight any legal action you try to take against him, and also that his mum is a lawyer. However, he is very sorry that everyone found out and that Jessica Clark has been making fun of you. So, as a gesture of goodwill, he would like to offer you some compensation.

Destroy this note.

"It was the HACKER!" Cammy whispered.

"He must've been at our gig and knew that it was Jessica who sabotaged us with the spoons!"

Just then I spotted ladybird girl in the middle of the corridor, looking up at the screen with a little smile on her face.

And then I spotted her hat.

"Cammy, LOOK!" I said. "Look at her hat!"

Ladybird girl had at least six of our band badges on her little red hat.

"Oh wow!" said Cammy. "Wait. Do you think that *she* might be the hacker?"

Just then she spotted us staring at her.

Ladybird girl gave a wave. And then she winked and disappeared into the crowd.